LF

D1488585

THE
SHADOW

THE
SHADOW

by Benito Pérez Galdós

translation and introduction
by Karen O. Austin

OHIO UNIVERSITY PRESS
Athens, Ohio

Library of Congress Cataloging in Publication Data

Pérez Galdós, Benito, 1843-1920.
The shadow.

Translation of La sombra.
Bibliography: p.
I. Title.
PZ3.P416Sh 1980 [PQ6555] 863 .5 80-10549
ISBN 0-8214-0553-5

Introduction ©1980 by Karen O. Austin
Printed in the United States of America

INTRODUCTION

Benito Pérez Galdós

Benito Pérez Galdós was born in Las Palmas in the Canary Islands on May 10, 1843. The youngest son in a large, mother-dominated family, he attended local schools until his graduation from the Colegio de San Agustín in 1862. There were a number of English people living there, and he may have learned some of the language from them; several of his biographers have claimed that he was educated at an English school there, though there are no records that would support such a contention. His artistic inclinations were apparent from an early age and he produced numerous drawings, some of which received honorable mention at an exhibition in Santa Cruz de Tenerife in 1862.

In 1862, he went to Madrid to study law at the University. He quickly discovered the attractions of the Madrilenian streets and cafés, however, and although he continued to register at the University for some years, it was largely an attempt to avoid having to return to Las Palmas. His enthusiasm for Madrid was overwhelming, and with the fervor typical of converts he came to know it far better than its native inhabitants. He became the art and drama critic for the newspaper *La Nación* in 1865, and began a steady output of essays; he wrote several plays as well, but none of them were produced, and he abandoned active involvement in the drama for many years.

Galdós seems to have discovered Balzac during his first trip to Paris in 1867. The encounter with the French novelist's works had considerable influence on the young Spanish journalist, and his commitment to the novel and to Realism effectively date from this point. This is by no means to say that the Canary-born author was an imitation, a reflection of Balzac. Galdós had his own style, his own aesthetic and ethical stance, and his own peculiarly Spanish frame of reference, with all its attendant historical and cultural orientation.

La sombra, or *The Shadow,* was written, according to Galdós' own statement, in 1866 or 1867, although it was not published until 1870, when it appeared in serial form in *La Revista de España,* a newspaper whose staff he joined in that year. It was on his return from Paris that he began *La Fontana de Oro,* his second novel, also published in 1870. The action of the latter novel takes place against the backdrop of the political machinations and upheavals of Fernando VII's repressive reign (1814-1833), and, together with the next novel, *El Audaz* (1871), is basically didactic in intent. The author's purpose in his choice of period is twofold: he seeks first to explain the problems of the current political situation by exploring their causes in the immediate past; and, by referring to events still fresh and vivid in the minds of his readers, he urges them to practice greater tolerance in the future.

Galdós himself had firsthand familiarity with many of the events he described, and they confirmed him in an essentially liberal outlook. On several occasions he took an active part in politics, serving as the representative in Parliament for Guayama, Puerto Rico, in 1886, and later, in 1907 and 1910, for Madrid. His close contact with practical politics was not a very happy one and, while he remained a liberal, he was a somewhat disenchanted one. *La Fontana de Oro* and *El Audaz* are the precursors of the *Episodios Nacionales,* a series of 46 novels which are rather more fictionalized history than historicized fiction. Encompassing Spanish history from 1805 (the Battle of Trafalgar) to about 1879, they are lively and straightforward, although there is a move in the final *episodios* to a fabular, allegorical approach reflective of his political disillusionment.

At the same time that he was writing the *Episodios Nacionales,* Galdós undertook narrative of a different sort, thesis novels criticizing various aspects of Spanish society. *Doña Perfecta* (1877), which received immediate European acclaim and remains one of his best known and most widely translated works, deals with a well-educated, progressive young man from Madrid who comes into immediate conflict with the inhabitants of a conservative, rural town, a situation which ends in tragedy. *Gloria* (1877) pits Catholic against Jew, with religious intolerance equally distributed on both sides. In *Marianela* (1878), the problem of true reality is taken up when a blind boy's sight is restored, thanks to medical advances, and his whole world and that of a young girl is unhappily reversed. The last of this particular group, termed the *novelas de la primera época,* is *La familia de León Roch* (1878), in which an intellectual once again encounters religious bigotry and intransigence. Although Galdós has a definite ax to grind, these novels remain eminently readable. His types, though representative, never fall into the sin of caricature, and his generalizations escape the excesses of abstraction. Most importantly, his innate sense of balance and proportion insures that all his potentially melodramatic characters and situations remain human, neither blindly to be praised nor ruthlessly to be condemned.

La familia de León Roch already shows a tendency away from the thesis novel and towards a greater interest in matters aesthetic and the problems of life in contemporary society. This tendency is more pronounced in the *serie contemporánea,* as he called the following novels. To Balzac's influence is added that of Emile Zola and the Naturalist schools, but in both instances there are sensible modifications, techniques and methods being adapted to a unique and essentially Spanish view of reality as that view had filtered down through Cervantes, the picaresque novel, Goya, and others. In *La desheredada* (1881), a girl is unable to relinquish her belief that she is in fact of noble birth, and eventually becomes a prostitute. Heredity is a strong factor, and the background, from the initial scene in an insane asylum, makes ample use of the wretched conditions of lower-class Madrid, a backdrop also used for another novel of illusion and insanity, *El doctor Centeno* (1883). Moral and sexual decadence figure in *Tormento* (1884) and *Lo prohibido* (1885), and in *La de Bringas* (1884) there is once again the obsessive and ill-fated upwards social drive of a *petite bourgeoise.*

Naturalistic intent is not overpowering even in this period, however. In 1882, Galdós published *El amigo Manso,* which, while dealing with the personal problems of its protagonist, also treats in an original manner the relationship of an author to his fictional creation. In this, it is well within the Cervantine tradition, and is generally considered to be the inspiration of Unamuno's universally recognized *Niebla* (1914). Experimentation with the recourses available to a writer of fiction fascinated Galdós, who returned to his first love, the drama, in 1892, while he continued with the novels. He incorporated dramatic techniques such as stage directions and extensive dialogues directly into many of his works, perhaps most remarkably in *La incognita* (1889) and *Realidad* (1889), geminate novels in which a single event is viewed from widely divergent points of view in an effort to ascertain the deeper truth and reality of the matter. Exclusive dialogue was to reappear as a favored technique in *La loca de la casa* (1892) and *El abuelo* (1897), where spiritual issues of a higher nature again take precedence over mere pedestrian fact.

Frequently considered by modern critics to be his masterpiece, *Fortunata y Jacinta* (1886-87) gives plentiful evidence of this growing penchant for an investigation into the more profound meaning of things. Jacinta, a refined, rather fragile woman of the upper-class, and Fortunata, lower-class but vibrant and passionate, compete for the affections of Jacinta's shallow husband, Juanito Santa Cruz. Though they rarely come into contact, their lives revolve about one another, and their polarity achieves a balance when Fortunata, dying, gives Juanito's child to her barren competitor.

Rivaling *Fortunata y Jacinta* for preeminence is *Angel Guerra* (1890-91), in which two female figures, Leré and Dulcenombre, are again used to suggest a composite ideal, and in which religion, in the early works is seen primarily in the more negative aspects of orthodox religiosity, is viewed in a much more positive light. This changing attitude of the author is accompanied by incidents that suggest a possible entrance of the genuinely miraculous into the stuff of the novel, greatly at odds with the distorted hallucinations of the earlier, more naturalistic works. A similar possibility is put forward in *Misericordia* (1897), where Galdós seeks to examine the nature of true charity and compassion. The novels of this period represent a pinnacle in Galdós' artistic creation, for they retain the best of the earlier works in technique, characterization, description and humor, while adding a dimensionality which far surpasses a simple symbolic overlay.

In his later years, Galdós applied himself with renewed vigor to the *Episodios* and to the drama. Although he was to write three final novels in the *serie contemporánea—Casandra* (1905), *El caballero encantado* (1909) and *La razón de la sinrazón* (1915)—they, like the final *episodios,* reflect his growing disillusionment and failing health, and in their abandonment to overt allegory they lack the charm and attraction of their predecessors. Galdós was beyond a doubt the greatest Spanish writer of his century, but he was until 1897 denied admission to the Royal Academy by its conservative members. Their refusal to recommend him likewise cost him the Nobel Prize. Distressed and embittered by his abortive endeavors in the political arena, and never particularly adept at handling finances and royalties, he spent his last years in blindness and relative poverty, largely supported by subscription. His popularity was confirmed upon his death on January 4, 1920, however, when he received a state funeral. Mourners from all sectors of Spanish society turned out by the thousands, and memorial services were held throughout the world, acknowledging the position he still holds: the greatest figure in Spanish letters since Cervantes.

The Shadow

The action of the novel, as the reader is in a position to reconstruct it at the end of the work, would appear simple enough. Anselmo, the son of a well-to-do family, is melancholic and highly variable in his emotions. His father arranges for him to marry a young woman named Elena, and he accedes to this plan. Although, as he himself points out, they had scarcely spoken to one another before the wedding, he soon thereafter falls madly in love with her; his already precarious mental balance is exacerbated by this new development in his life, and he careens from moments of ecstasy to deep depressions. He becomes wildly jealous, not altogether surprisingly, since he has never had occasion to reach a true appreciation of Elena's character or personality. He imagines the existence of a rival for her affections whom he sees personified in a sensual painting of Paris and Helen of Troy which hangs in one of the rooms of his house. The figure of Paris becomes quite real to Anselmo, and he imagines that it has disappeared from the canvas. He thinks he hears voices in his wife's room, and bursts in; the first time he does so he finds nothing, and apologizes to Elena for his behavior, but on a second occasion he seems to see a shadow escaping through her window and gives chase. His condition further deteriorates, and this shadow assumes form and substance as Anselmo's grip on reality weakens. He holds conversations with this figment of his imagination, and even believes he has fought a duel with him.

This creation of his disordered mind has a basis in fact, for a young man-about-town of dubious reputation, one Alejandro, is spending considerable time in the house, keeping Elena company. Whether there is anything culpable in their relationship is never clear, but his mere presence is enough to push Anselmo over the brink, and his irrational verbal attacks and wild behavior result in Elena's breakdown and death. Once she is dead, and the cause of his doubts thus effectively removed, Paris, the physical embodiment of his fears, disappears, and he is released from his obsession.

The Shadow is a noteworthy little novel for several reasons. As the author's first novel, it shows some of the romantic tendencies of the literature of his day, especially in its rather fantastic subject matter, for which reason it has been largely neglected by critics until recent years. It is, however, demonstrably a Realist work. A Realist author is expected, for example, to use language referential to the real world: if a writer employs the word *brick*, the reader has a right to assume that this is the sort of brick which he himself has often seen. It is this establishment of a common ground of shared experiences which results in the lengthy, detailed, and often tedious descriptive passages that abound in a Realist novel. Certainly, Galdós' description of Anselmo's living quarters, and Anselmo's own descriptions of his past surroundings, fit this requirement nicely. Furthermore, such a technique by no means excludes the use of these same objects as symbols, as is clearly evidenced by the simple necessity of using words to write of them, since they are all, of course, symbols by definition.

Realistic objectivity also requires an unbiased point of view, achieved in *The Shadow* by the coexistence of two narrators with opposing views, and to a lesser extent by the citing of public opinion on various aspects of the affair. The fantastic subject matter of the tale itself is no diriment impediment to Realism: one need only point to Bram Stoker's *Dracula*, wherein letters, diaries, newspaper clippings, and so forth are used to persuade the skeptical reader of the consequent truth of the extraordinary matters related. A Realist author has a perfect right to have both thesis and opinion, and to attempt to convince his reader of them: even the most impartial journalist must show some selectivity in the choice of the facts he presents, and this selection depends perforce on his own beliefs. The Realist author is limited, not in *what* he presents, but in *how* he presents it.

One may readily call to witness other elements commonly attendant in Realist works. There is in *The Shadow* the concern with the very real social problems of marriages arranged without sufficient prior acquaintance, and of the Spanish concept of honor, the latter of which is at the very root of Anselmo's worries, as Paris points out to him. Most readily apparent is Galdós' interest in the psychological factors and the medical background underlying the protagonist's mental aberration. Thus he refers to heredity as a partial cause, explaining through another character that Anselmo's father suffered similar delusions, although the latter's centered on persecution by a mythical creditor. Though some of the opinions offered towards the end of the work may strike the modern reader as naive, even bizarre, it should be remembered that Galdós was writing in the early dawn of the science of psychiatry, more than a quarter of a century before Freud began to publish. Within the historical context, then, his analysis shows an enlightened awareness of the latest theories and advances of his day, and his own personal observations demonstrate a great understanding of human nature and an insight into the workings of the mind.

In his preface to the first edition, Galdós states: "What I primarily wish to point out about this little work is that in it I took my first tottering steps, as the saying goes, in the tricky art of writing novels." In addition to providing practice with the Realist techniques and orientations we have just mentioned, Galdós became involved from the start with the intriguing possibilities of pure aesthetic creation, possibilities which were later to lead him to experimentation with the uses of dramatic techniques, extratemporal intrusions, and the like, all with the ultimate aim of revealing true reality.

From the standpoint of *The Shadow*, this probing of artistic recourses is centered in the use of several narrators and in the question of final authorship and veracity that this entails. From the outset, Galdós invests his protagonist with considerable artistic independence. There is present an unnamed character and narrator whom one presumes to be either Galdós or at the least his appointed spokesman within the work, who ought therefore to be the most authoritative figure in the book, and the one the reader should be able to believe in any case of doubt. This Galdós *persona* sets the scene, describing the surroundings in which Anselmo lives and giving us a picture of his character and reputation. Perhaps more importantly, he establishes a humorous and disbelieving attitude towards Anselmo's strange utterances, making of himself the representative of realism and rationality and inviting the reader to share his tongue-in-cheek approach to Anselmo's story.

The mood shifts, however, as Anselmo relates his strange history, gradually usurping the role of narrator. Comments and interjections from the Galdós *persona* become infrequent. The reader now gains all his information from the supposedly demented Anselmo, and more dependence is placed on his views as a result. As the principal narrator, Anselmo achieves a dignity and authority that would otherwise be denied him, and he moves from the merely ludicrous to the nearly tragic. When yet another character emerges, the shadowy being named Paris who gains increasing substance, the reader is forced to concede this shadow a certain validity and existence, for the influence he exerts over Anselmo is both obvious and crucial.

Anselmo's control over the direction of the narrative continues until the very end, when the Galdós *persona* again becomes active, attempting to reconstruct the events in the light of reality. One might expect a full-circle return at this point to the level of reality on which the novel started, in opposition to the fantastic, supernatural level on which Anselmo has operated. Yet Anselmo acknowledges the truth of every fact that the Galdós *persona* brings up: indeed, he was aware of the true sequence of events before he began his tale. And in spite of this, he elected to tell it as he did because, as he says, "...to give my adventure more truth, I recount it as it happened to me, which is to say, backwards." The Cervantine atmosphere is detectable throughout, and makes for a vague uneasiness as to the precise nature of reality.

The case for Galdós' *locum tenens* in the novel possessing beyond doubt the solution to the matter is weakened by this relinquishment of narrative direction, and is brought into further question by several other factors. First and most significantly, this surrogate Galdós was not present when the events of the story actually took place: the only source on which he may rely, other than on Anselmo's own report, is hearsay, but he is quick to note that the truth is not known. Further, the Galdós *persona* several times interrupts Anselmo's discourse to query a specific detail, thereby implying that he has, unconsciously, been taking the rest of the account seriously. As an aside, one should also note that the Galdosian narrator's case for dementia at the end rests on Paris' being Anselmo's visualization of the real person, Alejandro; but while Alejandro may well be the inception of Paris, they are certainly not identical, for Anselmo repeatedly sees and converses with Paris when Alejandro is nowhere present. Finally, the Galdós *persona* twice asks Anselmo, at the last, if, after Elena's death, the figure of Paris returned to the canvas whence he sprang, obviously considering it a point of some import. On neither occasion does Anselmo give him an answer, however. At the novel's finish, as the original narrator is leaving Anselmo's apartments, he starts to go back to ask Anselmo yet again, but then decides to drop the matter. This, if he truly wishes to tie up loose ends, is no way to set about it. The reader is given a perfectly enlightened, scientific explanation of the phenomenon, but is left in some doubt as to whether that explanation is totally satisfactory, even to the author.

These various motifs and ideas are, as noted, independent of, but not contradictory of, the basic tenets of literary Realism. And their presence here in the first of such an enormous production of novels is of vital importance to any student of Galdós, for while they are temporarily eclipsed in the early novels in favor of more traditional Realism, they contain the seeds developed in the later and most mature of his works. As with the later books, the artistic excursions of *The Shadow* combine to form its rich, multidimensional and multifaceted world, lifting it above the flat realm of the scientific and rational and indicating already many of the directions Galdós' interest was to take as he pursued his novelistic quest for the deeper truth.

SELECTED BIBLIOGRAPHY

Berkowitz, H. Chanon. *Benito Pérez Galdós: Spanish Liberal Crusader.* Madison: University of Wisconsin Press, 1948.

Bosch, Rafael. *"La sombra* y la psicopatología de Galdós." *Anales Galdosianos,* 7 (1971), 21-42.

Cardona, Rodolfo, ed. *La sombra.* New York: W.W. Norton and Co., 1964.

Casalduero, Joaquín. *"La sombra." Anales Galdosianos,* 1 (1966), 33-38.

Casalduero, Joaquín. *Vida y obra de Galdós.* Madrid: Editorial Gredos, 1970.

Clavería, Carlos. "Sobre la veta fantástica en la obra de Galdós." *Atlante,* London, 1 (1953), 78-86, 136-43.

Correa, Gustavo. "El diabolismo en las novelas de Pérez Galdós." *Bulletin Hispanique,* 65 (1963), 284-96.

Correa, Gustavo. *El simbolismo religioso en las novelas de Pérez Galdós.* Madrid: Editorial Gredos, 1974.

Gullón, Germán. *"La sombra,* novela de *suspense,* y novela de fantasía." *Actas del Primer Congreso Internacional de Estudios Galdosianos.* Madrid: Editora Nacional, 1977, 351-56.

Gullón, Ricardo. *Galdós, novelista moderno.* Madrid: Editorial Gredos, 1973.

Montesinos, José F. *Galdós.* Madrid: Editorial Castalia, 1968.

Rovettá, Carlos. *"La Sombra,* novela primigenia de Galdós." *Nosotros,* 7 (1943), 184-96.

Turner, Harriet S. "Rhetoric in *La Sombra:* the Author and his Story." *Anales Galdosianos,* 7 (1971), 5-19.

CHAPTER I: DOCTOR ANSELMO

I

One should begin at the beginning, that is, by telling the reader just who this don Anselmo is; by telling him of his life, his habits, by speaking of his character and appearance, without omitting the fact that everyone who knew him considered him to be stark raving mad. This opinion was general, unanimous, deeply rooted, and the frequent flashes of genius of that incomparable man, his moments of good sense and eloquence, the affable courtesy with which he lent himself to the telling of the most curious events of life, making discreet use in his narrations of his prodigious imagination, were insufficient to belie it. They said that he did idiotic things, that his life was a series of innumerable follies, and that he became engrossed in strange and incomprehensible pursuits not undertaken by anyone else, in sum, that he was a strange fellow who had never been known to do anything right, the way the rest of us normally do things.

Few people had anything to do with him; only a bare handful of persons might call themselves his friends; the majority scorned him, and all those who knew nothing of his previous life, and who did not know how to see what there was of a singular and extraordinary nature in that spirit, viewed him with contempt and even with repugnance. It is not easy to say if there was some justice in this, nor is it an easy matter to come to an exact appreciation of that man, putting him amongst the greatest or assigning him a place next to the greatest fools born of human mother. He himself will reveal to us in the course of this narrative some few things that will be useful in judging him as he deserves.

He lived on the fourth floor of an ugly, ill-proportioned house, which he never left unless urgent business called him out. The house was in such shape that, in a less hurried century, popular fantasy would have furnished it with all the participants of a witches' Sabbath.

In the present period the only witch to be found there was one doña Monica, housekeeper, maid, and general administrator.

The doctor's room resembled one of those laboratories that we have seen in more than one novel, and that have served as backdrop in a quantity of Dutch pictures. It was lit by the same melancholy lamp with which in theatres and paintings we see illuminated the cadaverous face of Doctor Faustus, of Master Klaes, of the medieval glassblowers, of the good Marquis de Villena, and of the manufacturers of poisons and drugs in the Italian republics. This made our hero appear very nearly a practitioner of black magic or a Jew, but he was nothing of the sort, although in his house, fantastic as we shall see, there were to be seen hanging from the ceiling those strange animals that seem to bring to life one of Teniers' dreams, wheeling across the vault in confused formation.

Here was no gothic vault, nor gracefully designed windows, nor the dark background, the mysterious light effects by which the craftsmanship of paint-ing presents us with the hiding-places of those chemists who, wrapped in illus-trious cobwebs, lean perpetually over a scrawl-filled tome. Doctor Anselmo's sitting-room was a commonplace room of the sort we all live in, composed of four uneven walls and a crumbling ceiling, in whose surface the plaster, falling from the carelessness of time and the neglect of the tenants, had left huge holes. There was no wallpaper nor any wall covering other than that of the spiders, weaving their intricate patterns from corner to corner.

On the main wall of the fireplace was a skeleton who had not lost the good humor of the grave, so widely stretched in frightful laughter were his toothless jaws, and the oddity of his appearance was increased by the kettle that the doctor had put on his skull, doubtless for lack of a better place to hang it.

To the side was a wooden bookshelf with countless trinkets, principal amongst which were some broken vases of inestimable merit and pieces of the crudest domestic earthenware. A stuffed, half-rotted bird enhanced with the brilliant color of its last feathers this unwieldy piece of furniture, next to which a straw-stuffed snake trailed over the wall the curves of its body, its scales still giving off a weak iridescence. Close by hung a suit of armor, as rusty as though since the time of Roland—its owner, perhaps—it had not been cleaned. Some other blades and firearms hung there together with a huge frying pan, whose handle touched the feet of a figure of Christ, one of those that, with livid body, twisted members, anguished face, black hands, bloodstained shroud and cross, have been invented by Spanish art for the terror of the devout and the astonishment of sextons. The Christ was yellow, dark, shiny, rigid as a stuffed animal: it had no shape; the face was disfigured by the vermilion, and the feet were lost in the folds of a large decorative knot that must doubtless have been a place of pilgrimage for every fly in the neighborhood, for they had left indelible traces of their passing there. Elsewhere there peeped forth some conch shells, a picture of some saint or other, mother-of-pearl shells, two pistols, and a rosary of aquamarine beads tangled in a branch of coral, blackened by the dust. Two large spurs and a saddle hung from another spike next to grimy clothes in whose folds could be seen the neck of a guitar with a fine inlay of mother-of-pearl and ivory.

It was dented, and a single string, mute witness today of its past grandeur, could give the present generation an echo of past harmonies. Some army boots lay tossed about on the floor next to the guitar, while opposite hung a dress coat and waistcoat from the last century, both articles full of holes and stains. A three-cornered hat appeared on a round jar with a spout that did service as a head, and there was a deformed lamp in the shape of a candlestick that stained with the remnants of its secular oil a prie-Dieu elegantly worked, but so multilated that it had scarcely any form. On a nearby wall was a clock that had stopped fifty years past. Its works were the general headquarters of the spiders, and its enormous lead weights, fallen with a crash twenty-five thousand nights before, had broken a stool, a jar, and a Child Jesus, and were lying motionless on the floor with the majesty of two meteorites.

The person who entered that room could not escape a certain feeling of stupefaction, for the scant light from the lamp produced the strangest effects; as well as the odds and ends we have described, countless machines of peculiar and complicated design occupied the room. Stills that looked like glass snakes spread their spirals over enormous retorts, their bellies warmed by a constantly heated burner. The disk of an electric machine reverberated, and the whole machine constantly threatened us with its disagreeable manifestations. The dull noise of the flames of the fireplace, the crackling of the hot coals, like the far-off vibration of a mysterious instrument, the odor of the acids, the emanation of the gasses, the asthmatic wheezing of the bellows, laboring tiredly like a sick lung, all this produced indescribable anxiety and nausea in the spectator.

When this writer had the honor of penetrating the studio, sitting-room, or laboratory of Dr. Anselmo, his astonishment was considerable, and he cannot but confess that, alongside the astonishment, he felt a certain terror, alleviated only by the idea that that man was the most affable and inoffensive of beings. Besides, who did not know that don Anselmo was no necromancer, that he practiced none of the diabolic arts of antiquity? Scarcely anyone took his work seriously, and in the neighborhood he was held to be rather more a fool or an idiot than a man of moderate intelligence, with some vestiges of common sense. Nonetheless, he was engrossed in that endless task, which never produced any results, and to judge by the gravity with which he fanned his furnaces and by the anxious attention with which he ran the green and red liquids through the glass of the stills, he was dealing with great and transcendent problems.

His fondness for Chemistry was new; only recently had he turned to a consideration of simples and compounds. He had almost always employed the greater part of his time in reading all sorts of books, provided no imprudent individual came by to amuse himself listening to his picturesque narratives, remarkable for their brilliance and great flights of fancy. His conversation always turned on facts of his own life, which he brought up on any pretext. He never needed to have his arm twisted, and what he related was generally so odd that many people thought he had invented the whole. When he thought of his past, he would look at all those trinkets hanging there, and would laugh with gentle sadness, saying:

"I have been young too; I have been a courtier, an artist, a painter, a musician; I have travelled extensively, I have been a lover, I have been pursued, I have fought duels, I know the world, I have loved life and I have despised it, I have loved and hated violently."

On one occasion, after speaking in this manner, he pressed his yellow, thin, rigid finger against the only string of the guitar, which vibrated with a dull moan, its quivering shaking off all the dust that twenty years of quietude had deposited on it. He fell silent, remaining for a long time thoughtful and staring fixedly at the red liquid circulating through the glass intestine, decanting its subtle essence from one receptacle to another.

It was in those moments of silence, interrupted only by the faint vibration of the string, the noise of the flames, and that incomprehensible, solemn sound of all mysterious places, that the strange objects in the scholar's lodgings caused me the greatest terror. It seemed to me as though it were all alive and in motion: that the dress-coat was moving, as though its skirts covered a body and its sleeves encased arms.

I also thought I saw the three-cornered hat wagging from side to side, as though the jar holding it up had brains full of intelligence and good humor; I thought I saw the boots spurring the prie-Dieu, and the conch shells beating against one another like castanets tied to the fingers of an Andalusian hand. The skeleton seemed to be yawning, and the kettle fell down to his eyes, tilting to one side to give him a droll expression; he seemed to put his left foot forward, like someone about to dance, and to put his two hands on his waist, which fit in his two fingers.

I imagined the clock was running with the speed and diligence of a machine trying to catch up in minutes with the years it had sat idle-handed, or rather, idle-wheeled; I heard the tick-tock of the works, and I thought I saw the pendulum swing from side to side, striking at all the stuffed birds, that tried to fly, moving with difficulty the sparse feathers of their rotted wings, and finally, in the midst of all that uproar, I thought I saw the Christ twist his arms and neck, stretching, with an expression on his face of supreme boredom.

Let us introduce this person.

Don Anselmo would appear to be an uncommon type, one of those people more often seen in the artificial world of the novel and the theatre than on life's stage, where we all form that huge social group which seems to us today a signal vulgarity, and which may in fact be one. Don Anselmo, upon being introduced in that odd scene we have described, in the midst of so many peculiar props, with this medieval paraphernalia and the look of a sorcerer or a seeker of the philosopher's stone, would seem to be a character altogether foreign to present-day society, a senseless, purposeless ideological creation rather than the faithful portrait of the average man. These beliefs vanish when one discovers that don Anselmo was a man of so unromantic an aspect, so everyday and commonplace, that no one would pay any attention to him were it not for his famous manias and eccentricities and his absurd conversation.

He was a badly preserved old man, thin and somewhat sickly, a bit on the short side, with one of those insignificant faces that seems no different from that of the man next door unless one studies it with a formal observation and particular interest. Only when he laughed could one see in his face traces of an unusual liveliness. At such moments his little sunken eyes shone and his mouth, endowed with the greatest mobility we have known, used a more varied and expressive system of signs than words themselves. He limped on one foot, why we do not know, and he did not have the full use of his left hand; his voice was hoarse and cracked, and when he walked, he went in such a direct line, so straight-ahead and absent-minded, that he bumped into everyone. He seemed to have a fixed idea stuck in his mind, an idea that gave him no respite, that kept him from attending to anything else, and when walking he could be seen to become agitated, change color, gesture, working all the muscles in his face like someone engaged in a heated conversation with invisible interlocutors. Speaking to himself was, for him, a constant exercise rather than a habit; his life, a never-ending monologue.

His dress was unremarkable here, where there is a museum of the ridiculous in constant exhibition on the streets. If his frock coat was the object of curiosity because of the exorbitant height of the lapels, shiny with the grease and wear of fifteen years, we can find in none of the chroniclers who have dealt with this extraordinary man anything to suggest that the public noticed the roominess of his vest, where four doctors could have fit comfortably, nor in the never before seen shape of his necktie, which at times, as is the case with many scholars and people who talk to themselves, would twist around until the knot was at the back of his neck.

The simplicity and purity of his habits was exemplary: he ate little, drank less, and slept, in the few free hours his fantasy allowed him, fairly soundly, always dreaming as much as when he was awake. Most of his time he spent in study, which according to many people did him no good at all, but rather, on the contrary, left in worse snarls than ever the tangle of follies in his head.

He lived on a certain modest pension from some place or other and on the few coins he had gotten from the sale of the last remnants of his fortune. He seemed, in fine, one of those hermits of science who waste away, victims of their zeal, and who turn to spirit, losing bit by bit even the common outer shell of ordinary men and turning into fools who are good for little but making idle people laugh. His manner, his temperament, his personality, was all narration. When he related something, it was he, it was Dr. Anselmo in his genuine form and exact expression. His accounts usually resembled the supernatural, fabulous undertakings of the knights errant, though they took as their basis events from real life, which he raised to the level of the marvelous with his flights of fancy.

When relating these things, always having to do with some period of his life, he brought into play the most fanciful recourses of rhetoric and a wealth of erudite trivia that he tossed out here and there with the greatest casualness. His style did not lack artistry, being in general varied, lively, and picturesque.

From all of this, the reader may think we are dealing with some literary figure abandoned by the critics and out of popular favor, one of those who, unable to use their life in the exercise of their art and the full enjoyment of glory, give way to misery and despair. No; Dr. Anselmo was no writer nor, to the best of our knowledge, did anything ever issue from his pen other than a few badly kept accounts of his household losses and some memorandum or other proving his rights to his pension. He was a man with an insane idea firmly fixed in his head. Perhaps by knowing some of the details of his life and by attending to the incident he himself will relate to us, we may discover how that intelligence should have become so deranged and how so many and such wild images should have become lodged in his brain, next to such discriminating judgements, how such stupidity should co-exist with such great concepts, that appear to be the fruit of the sanest and most cultivated understanding.

The gentleman in question had had a very stormy youth, and from his earliest years was seen to be subject to violent emotions, a disordered imagination, fluctuating conduct, and changes from depression to activity that gave him a reputation as an unhinged man of little sense. They say that he spent whole weeks withdrawn from people, sad, bored as a saint, lost in vain ecstasies from which not even his friends could lure him forth. At other times his animation and joy were so great that they bordered on the delirious, it being difficult then to avoid his antics. But this would last only a short time, and he was soon to be seen again, solitary and abstracted, one of those wooden saints who look to heaven and stretch out a finger as though in expectation of a voice from above. It was in one of these periods that his father's death found him, leaving him heir to a considerable fortune: amongst other things, a magnificent house where the old man, a great art collector, had accumulated a multitude of fine Renaissance works. His family was one of the noblest of Andalusia: His last name was Afán de Ribera, being, in the maternal line, a branch of the Silíceos, due to which he could take pride in being a relative of the archbishop of the same name.

When describing the palace left him by his father, the doctor used the most brilliant colors; he made it out to be such a fantastic thing that it was unbelievable, and one could not help but think that the narrator's imagination had been the principal architect of such a beautiful abode.

My hero married a young woman of whose beauty he always spoke pompously. No one knows what happened in that marriage, and if what we are going to hear from the lips of the doctor himself is true, then we must admit that the case is strange and worthy of being placed amongst the most curious adventures ever to have taken place. Reliable sources state that, in the months he was married, our character's absentmindedness and eccentricity became extreme: he avoided human companionship altogether, seeking out solitary places, sometimes overcome by unquenchable anger, sometimes sunk in a profound melancholy, a sort of somnambulism which made him look like a man out of his senses. Rarely was he seen with his wife, to whom he showed not even the scant courtesies of the most intractable of husbands. He quarreled with his parents-in-law and did a thousand stupid things until finally malicious gossip, eager to know what was going on, entered his house and left no one with honor.

The truth is not known; Elena, for such was his wife's name, died a few months after their marriage, and it was then that Anselmo began to be the absurd figure we now know. He never again had calm, clear judgement, being from that moment on the man of extravagant and incoherent acts, more incomprehensible as time went on, wrapped up in his internal dialogues and always agitated by the insane idea that, little by little, came to form part of his mental constitution.

He lost his fortune, not just through carelessness, but because a relative of his began an insignificant lawsuit, and the members of the legal profession took such advantage of it that within a short time all the parties to it wound up in poverty. Some people said: "He is a great philosopher; see with what resignation he withstands the blows of fortune." Others said: "He is a crazy man; look with what indifference he lets his business matters slide." His stoicism was the butt of jokes. One person wanted to help him, feeling sorry for his misfortune; but it appears he was proud and not inclined to take charity. There were also some young men so naive that they thought he had begun a new philosophical system that would astound the world. This was due to the fact that after he had become poor he had gone up into the top of the attic, where he lit a lamp and began to read voraciously night after night without rest. But seeing that there was never any outcome from all that unceasing work, every-one found him increasingly mad. People who previously had been fond of him or had pitied him now fled from him, and only a very few persons went to hear him recount his wondrous adventures, which he had no doubt dreamed up, for there was no one whose role in society could have been more passive.

The title of doctor was no academic degree, as with most scholars; rather, it was a nickname with which his friends liked to satirize his erudite habits. Those who went to hear him relate his stories were not without good taste, for these latter were an astonishing web of deeds improbable, but of great interest, and so enlivened by picturesque digressions that, dealt with and written by a fairly adept pen, they may perhaps be read with pleasure. They referred in general to apparitions of some shadow that came to stroll through this world with the greatest impertinence, and he presented it as the symbolic representa-tion of some idea; he was fond of all sorts of symbols, and in his stories there was always a multitude of supernatural beings who formed a kind of modern mythology.

In all of this the erudition he had acquired in his assiduous reading played considerable part, for he was like a set of files in which everything is jumbled, without system or order. Who knows! Perhaps if there had been a catalogue in that head, Dr. Anselmo might have been one of the most extraordinary tal-ents alive.

III

The doctor continued to stare at that diabolic machine with the abandon-ment or unconcern that show on a person's face when his thoughts are far from the place where his eyes rest.

One would think that the result of the experiment was unimportant to him, that he was indifferent to the scientific truth with which the liquid circulated through the tube.

"But why did you go in for Chemistry?" I asked him, sure that the scientist would give me no categorical reply.

"To tie up that mad woman, my imagination," he answered, "to contain her and force her to torture me no longer. I always have to keep busy with something: reading distracted me a little, but I finally tired of that. Not long ago I saw things in certain books that attracted my attention and that I didn't understand. 'I'm going to see what that's all about,' I said. 'I need to get in-volved in experiments.' I bought those gadgets and I started blowing up the fire and making observations. A nomenclature and a manual were enough to distract me for a few days. But this is nothing more than a pastime: I cultivate my curiosity, though without any positive fruit. Let no one expect any scientific advance from all this. The truth is that as long as I heat my machine and decompound this rot-gut, I don't think about anything else, and I get along all right that way."

"The mad woman, always the mad woman!" I replied to him. "The truth is that imagination, which you're very right to call as you do, if you would just subdue her a little, far from tormenting you, could be a prolific source of creation, whose importance you more than anyone should recognize. Why didn't you apply yourself to the arts?"

"Oh! To cultivate the arts," he said, turning his back on the apparatus, "one needs an imagination which is held in check within the natural limits, an imagination that is a faculty with the attributes of a faculty, and not a sickness, as it is in me, an aberration, an organic vice. That precious faculty, though it may be overly abundant in some, never manages to dominate the individual to the point of imposing a second life on him: it is not, as it is in me, fully half of one's being. I don't know why I came into the world with this monstrosity; I'm not a man, or rather, I'm like those repugnant, deformed men you see around with improbable limbs that shame the Creator. My imagination is not a power that creates, that gives birth to organized and complete intellectual beings; it is a frantic power in constant motion, forever producing visions and more visions. It works like the never-ending worm gear. What comes out of it is like the thread that comes out of a hank of wool and twists around, spinning endlessly, never coming to a stop. This thread of mine never runs out, and as long as I'm alive, I'll carry that spool around in my head, a machine of pain that whirls without cease."

"It's true," I said mechanically, astonished that in his madness he should have been able to express so well and in such a picturesque manner the deplorable state of his brain.

"I am a slave to this," he went on. "Ever since I was a child I have suffered the ravages of my imagination. In fifty years, she has made me live three hundred. Yes, the false sensations that I, although removed from the world, have experienced in my life, add up to the lives of six men; I have lived too much, because fantasy has added millions of days to my allotted time.

"That's torn it," I said to myself, while I nodded my head respectfully. "You've gotten him started up on his manias and you're stuck here for the night."

"I'm a unhappy man, the unhappiest of men," continued the doctor. "My misfortunes are unequalled in the world and resemble nothing of what we read. Other men are mortified within their own nature, while I in this respect am outside the common law of human grief, because my being is double: I have another being within me, another who accompanies me everywhere and is always telling me a thousand things that terrify me and keep me in a state of constant emotional fever. And the worst of it is that this fever does not consume me as fevers of the body do. On the contrary, it enlivens me; I feel as though this interior flame is regenerating my nature, predisposing it to be mortified every day."

"It's odd," I said, understanding nothing of all this business about an interior flame, and a double being, and an endless worm gear.

"I don't see anyone like me anywhere," he went on. "The only ones I can call brother are the Spanish mystics who have lived a complete ideal life along with their actual life. They had an obsession, another *I* in their heads. Sometimes I've thought of the existence of a parasite who occupies the region of our brain, who lives in there, feeding on our vital juices and thinking with our thoughts."

"Explain that a little more," I said, satisfied to see don Anselmo start out on one of his quirks that looked as though it were going to be very amusing.

"It's just a vague idea....If I could exteriorize myself, express everything that's in me, a lot of people who laugh at me today would be astounded."

"Oh! If you were to write your memoirs, don Anselmo," I said, affecting great seriousness so that he should have no misgivings, "your equal would not be found amongst the ancients or the moderns."

"That's so," replied don Anselmo, whose eyes were alive with sudden brilliance. "No one would equal me. My life has been a universal compendium of all human life, hasn't it?"

"Ah! Without a doubt. Who could fail to believe it?"

"You, who have heard me recount some incidents, will understand. Is it not true that there is nothing more marvelous than my marriage? You don't remember that novel occurrence I told you of, when I found myself in the presence of the strangest phenomenon ever to present itself to human observation?"

"I don't remember what you're talking about."

"My marriage, yes; I told you about it. What they said at the time was a tissue of lies. No one knew the truth of that strange event."

"You haven't told me a blessed thing about it," I said, remembering that, in spite of his frankness and loquacity, he had never spoken, except very obscurely, of that mysterious matter.

"You mean I never told you? I would have sworn I told you every detail just the other night."

"I assure you I don't know a thing about it."

"I didn't tell you the business of my wife, of that man..., of that demon...?"

"I don't know any of it."

"I haven't told you about my palace?"

"About the palace, yes, though only in passing," I said, remembering the fantastic picture of his house that the doctor so frequently painted.

"Oh, it was stupendous, marvelous! My father had a great love for the arts. What beautiful things, what jewels!"

10

"Yes, it must have been magnificent," I repeated, to spur him on to talk and amuse myself with the always majestic overflow of his fertile verbosity.

"It seems to me I'm still there," he said in a sort of ecstasy, "and I see my wife walking slowly, majestically, the way she always walked; to go in there, to close the door; I imagine I hear the noise of her clothes when they dropped, the sound of her bulky amber necklace as it was dropped onto the tray of the jewel case."

"Oh, go on, go on."

"Midnight is full of imaginings. She would pass in front of me, leaving a sort of trail of light. I wouldn't be asleep, I was on the alert, always with my ear cocked for that abominable voice."

"For Elena's voice?"

"No, no," he said furiously, "for the voice of....The blood ran from the wound...."

"Your wife was wounded, no doubt."

"No, he was; but that didn't keep him from showing me that infamous smile and that demoniacal look."

"I see that this is a complicated matter. Is there some person in all this whom I don't know about?"

"Oh yes, you know him, everybody knows him; he's always around. I see him every day. He was here a few nights ago."

"Who?"

"Him...but I'm going to tell you about it properly," he said, like someone who decides, after hesitating a long time, to make an important revelation. "You must have heard them talk at the time about my wife, about me. You probably heard a thousand idiotic things that were a long way from the truth. The pure truth is what I'm going to tell you now."

Dr. Anselmo began to speak, relating his strange history with enchanting profuseness. He lost no opportunity to demonstrate his eloquence; he described places in such a detailed and lively manner that one was captivated by his language. There was, nevertheless, a certain vagueness and confusion in the tale, and one had to adjust to his peculiar style to find the mysterious method he doubtless had. At first, as his imagination was running free, he rambled hither and thither; he interwove his account with maxims of his own devising, with valuations that had at times an astonishing originality and at other times displayed a candor close to folly. Needless to say, there was a great deal of fiction in it all, and in the descriptions, especially, he let his tongue run on thoughtlessly. It made one laugh to hear him describe his palace which, had it been as he made it out to be, would have had no equal in the most flourishing times of the arts. He let the vein of his learning flow freely when he reached this point, and reason could not curb him nor fear of appearing a liar hold him back. We do not know if the lies he related, and which we are going to transcribe, may

11

have, once arranged and put in order, some interest and semblance of common sense. They may turn out to be less insane than they appear at first; a thread of logic may show up in them, if one views them as a metaphysical creation. Perhaps, without the doctor himself knowing it, he had created a real fable, drawn from the bitterest period of his life, and he, without even suspecting it, by heaping a thousand lies and exaggerations into his story, had produced a little work of art, suitable to amuse and even to teach.

Shortly after he started, doña Monica came in, drawn by the warmth of the burner, the only fire in the house on winter nights. An openness worthy of patriarchal times obtained between the two; she was in the habit of pulling her chair up to the chemical apparatus and there, if she wasn't knitting, she would doze off with a peacefulness that the scholar could not observe without wonder. The emaciated cat, who looked as though he lived on chlorides and bromides, took a few steps through the room, like someone looking for something; he tried several places, settled down first on a book, then between two electric batteries, and finally, not liking either of these, came over to stretch out lazily between the good woman's feet.

Dr. Anselmo spoke as follows:

IV

"The first thing I intend to do is to give you an idea of what my palace was like, that palace I inherited from my father, the most enthusiastic collector of works of art who has ever existed. You will understand, when you become acquainted with that dwelling through my story, that anyone could expect happiness who had such means of satisfying it, and, at the same time, you will be astounded that I, a young man, gifted, though it ill becomes me to say so, and having estimable qualities, should have been the unhappiest being on earth. I married exactly as I wished; I married with complete satisfaction, full of enthusiasm, as in love as some beardless youth; my wife lived with me in that house until she died. You'll see how many things occurred in how few months. What an inquisition, what torments, what horrible mental torture! My house was built most mysteriously; there was nothing noteworthy about it on the outside, it was just one of those large houses left over in Madrid from the last century. All its marvels were on the inside: like the Arab alcazars, it was built either by great egotism or extreme reserve. My father carried out a dream there, he expressed everything he knew or had dreamed. I don't know what means he used in it nor what artists worked on it: it seemed something wrought by superior forces, a work sprung from the entrails of the earth, pushed forth by a diabolic will. Examined in detail, one could see there a sort of history and progress of the Arts throughout the ages. My father was a great ad-

12

mirer of antiquity and he wanted to represent it there; more than the delirium
of a powerful man, his house was the realization of an artist's dream, a delirium
symbolized in opulence, the true esthetic of millions. The jasper, the statues,
the bas-reliefs, the entering and departing lines, the mouldings and reflected
lights, the polished surface of the marble on the floor, that showed the entire
construction the other way 'round; the hollows, half dark, half luminous, of
the vaulted ceilings; the communication of the rows of arches, the geometric
cut of the lights, the breadth, the extension, the height, dazzled everyone entering that place for the first time. As one advanced, the spectacle was more
grandiose, and larger and more beautiful spaces offered themselves up to one's
contemplation. Each row of arches opened onto another enclosure, the cornices
intercepted one another, creating in their collisions more daring curves; the
arches shot the light back and forth, and that light, running from nave to nave
to illuminate ever larger spaces, seemed to reproduce on a growing scale a simple original concept, as though the refractive power of huge hidden mirrors
were at work there."

"It must have been really extraordinary," I said in the instant the doctor
stopped to catch his breath.

"I've only told you about the vestibule so far," he stated. "The rest...."

"Well, if that's nothing more than the vestibule, the rest must be beautiful
beyond the believing," I observed, unable to contain my consternation upon
seeing that my friend's lies and hyperboles knew no limits and exceeded what
we are accustomed to see in the most unsound and foolish of minds.

"Making one's way within," he continued, "one saw that ancient architecture dominated there, in all the variety of its most beautiful styles. The orna-
mentation was increasingly more lovely, without its profusion marring the
purity and harmony. First there was reflected there all the gracious simplicity
of the ancient temples of Athens; the same forms later acquired grace and elegance, modified by the hand of Ionic art. Farther on, the monotonous gleam
of the marble disappeared amongst the colors of the jasper, the gilding shone
in the acanthus leaves of the Corinthian capital, in the dentils and Grecian
frets. The human figure began to emerge in the keystones and triangular bas-
reliefs of the arches, in the monstrous hybrids that galloped across the frieze,
in the satyrs' heads, in the grotesque masks whose mouths, in a rictus of Ana-
creontic hilarity, spewed forth flowers and festoons. Farther along, the daugh-
ters of Caryae supported the severely adorned architrave, and now the human
figure appeared complete on the wall: the centaurs to one side, the amazons
to the other, continued their merciless fights. The nymphs, grouped on the
pediment, were crowning the head of the propitiary victim with roses. The At-
lantes, bent over, supported the roof, while on the bas-reliefs, magnificently
sculpted, were unfurled all the fables of the great righters of wrongs of Greece,
Hercules and Theseus. The figures were larger here, and the attitudes and forms

13

reached the limit of perfection of the ancient ideal. All the figures were divine, from Prometheus to Deianeira; all the monsters were men, from Polyphemus to Briareus...The quadruped himself, shaped by such an able chisel, had a sort of human expression. There Pegasus was a king who trots and flies, Cerberus a slave who barks through three mouths."

"But tell me: for there to have been so many things a huge amount of space would have been necessary," I said, piqued now by the enormous lies that the good don Anselmo wanted me to swallow, and eager to make him understand, in case he was trying to make fun of me, that I wasn't credulous enough to be taken in by all that nonsense.

The truth is that I was already somewhat dizzy from the pompous description of columns, jaspers, caryatids, and a thousand other odds and ends engendered in the mind of my friend. I knew, from what I had heard from some old people, that the so-called palace had nothing more outstanding than some mediocre old paintings, a few vases, and two or three old bookcases that don Anselmo's father had bought at public auction. I could not but be amazed that the deluded narrator should give such proportions to the artistic richness of the palace. I argued with him, finding it strange that here in Madrid there should exist such an enormous quantity of works of art, but he pretended not to understand and stuck to his obsession.

"In what appeared to be the center of the building," he added, with a gravity that tempted one to laughter, "and beneath the extremely high vaulted roof, there were innumerable works of statuary. There were groups representing the most famous deeds of Hellenic fable, and typical figures of incomparable beauty, well known, with the names of the divinities that have the most general attributes and representation. Together with the disasters of Ajax son of Oïleus and the horrors of Tantalus and Prometheus, there was a series of sculptures that portrayed the equally renowned adventures of the don Juan of Olympus. The poor victims of his intemperance were excessively elegant figures in whom one could see the effects of an identical passion, with differing features according to the various aspect with which the immortal deceiver had presented himself to them. They were all equally beautiful, without Europa's in any way resembling Latona, or Leda's having any similarity to Semele. Jupiter was always the same impudent god of lust, whether appearing in all his Olympic majesty, or turned into a bull or disguised with the feathers of a web-footed bird."

"What a devil that Jupiter was! The gentleman spared neither matrons nor maids," I observed, to see if jokes would force him to curb the flight of his disordered fancy.

It was to no avail. Don Anselmo went on:

14

"What I have described to you is really nothing more than a museum, the visible part of the house. The interior part, the inhabited part, was stranger yet."

"Stranger yet!" I said under my breath. "Stranger yet! Now we're in for it! Where is it all going to stop? If there's still more to this palace, this man is truly going to make my head spin tonight."

"I've only described the galleries!"

"Only galleries! Good Lord! What must there have been in the drawing rooms and bedrooms!" I exclaimed, alarmed.

"The great drawing room in no way resembled those magnificent constructions where architecture held sway. There was no style in its walls: detail dominated, and so many and so diverse were the precious articles accumulated there, that in vain would the most painstaking classifier try to describe and enumerate them."

"Now I'm for it," I thought.

"It was a museum of decorative arts, and here every object was a marvel, and the excellence of each disguised the confused but surprising perspective of the whole. Superb Renaissance furniture, with the richest cabinet work; Venetian cornucopias, clocks from the time of Louis Quinze, adorned with mythological figures; bas-reliefs of finest stucco portraying country hunts and dances; candelabras, busts, trivets and medallions were all massed on the wall; and all of this barely allowing one to glimpse the rich Flemish tapestry, whose colors, always fresh, revealed the designs of Teniers or Brueghel. Nor were there lacking those whimsical writing desks whose tiny compartments displayed little figures of consummate good taste, mosaics and inlays of different colored bits of wood, and to the side of these, occasional tables with porcelain plates, on which a delicate brush had given representation to an infinity of famous courtesans. Not far from these terrible beauties there were ancient and modern vases, cruets gilded with the filigree of the Arabic chisel and jars from India and Oceanus, where greenish lizards and imaginary predators, roughly worked, intertwined. Hindu idols with swollen bellies, deep navels and colossal ears laughed in one corner with the hilarity of a drunkard or a fool, and farther on, showy stuffed birds from America sat by African conch shells, branches of coral, a triptych from the Middle Ages, a Byzantine cross and Egyptian reliquaries that ...."

"Enough, enough," I shouted, rising from my chair. "You've already got my head whirling. That diabolical confusion of articles you possessed is beyond everything."

No doubt all the pots and broken crockery in his house struck the doctor as Egyptian vases and Byzantine crosses. He took no offense from my brusque interruption, and continued enthusiastically:

"To have looked for symmetry in that museum would have been to have destroyed its principal allure, which was its heterogeneousness and disorder. After the geometric delights of the galleries; after the cruel symmetry of the Doric and the dazzling regularity of the Corinthian, that hodge-podge of diverse objects...."

"Is not so great as the one you've got in your head," I said to myself, envying the luck of the cat, who was sleeping tranquilly without being obliged to admire the marvels of the Renaissance.

"That hodge-podge of objects, in some of which could be observed multiple orders, the agglomeration of pieces, furniture, vases, ornaments, with the stamp of different countries and different artists, the amalgam of beautiful, curious or rare things; all this delighted the understanding, overwhelmed until then by symmetry, and gave freedom to sight, previously subjugated by line. Here the objects joined with proper disorder, the infinite solutions of continuity, the complete absence of proportions, produced immense pleasure, and erasing every point of departure, spared the spectator the fatigue produced by the involuntary measuring which vision always succumbs to in the presence of architecture. Interiors, when they are beautiful, are like an abyss: they fascinate one's sight, and the spectator cannot forego mentally throwing out a plumb and tracing in space multiple lines with which his imagination tries to fathom the diameter of the arch, the height of the shaft of the column, and the radius of the vault. In this involuntary mental labor, produced by the harmony, the symmetry, the proportion, and the elegance, the mind tires and flags, between fatigue and amazement. When there are details but no style, when there is no point of view or key, one's sight does not grow tired, it rambles to and fro, it wavers, it loses itself; but it remains serene, because it does not try to measure or compare; it gives itself up to the confusion of the spectacle and, in straying, is saved."

At this point he stopped to catch his breath. I absorbed the lesson in perspective to the best of my ability, a lesson that seemed to me the height of confusion and befuddlement; but I must confess that the doctor inspired me with respect, and I dared say nothing that might offend him. Thus it is that, in spite of my boredom, I was forced to nod my head in assent. After resting for a moment, he went on:

"From this hall one passed into other rooms full of paintings."

"Yes...I understand: very pretty paintings. I've seen many paintings," I indicated, trying to force him to remove from me the new torment that I could feel coming on.

"In one of these rooms was to be found the key to the event I am going to relate. It seems to me I see him yet, that he is still there, with his elegant gaze, his perfidious, deceitful smile."

"Who was there?"

16

"I'll tell you. My father had a good collection of somewhat licentious pictures. There were a number of provocative, almost lewd nudes; there were 'gardens of love,' 'bacchanalia,' rural feasts and 'Venus at her bath.' The founder of this gallery was a great Epicurean and liked to enjoy himself among these mute witnesses and companions of his orgies. Among these pictures, there was one that stood out; it represented Paris and Helen reclining in a fresh grotto of the isle of Crannae. Beautiful was the face of the wife of Menelaus; but that of the young Trojan was more beautiful still. Such animation had the brush given him that he seemed to speak and to instill in Helen his perfidious thoughts. I always thought I saw something lifelike in that face, which at times, through some inexplicable illusion, seemed to move and laugh. It impressed everyone, and me especially. Remember this well, and you will have no difficulty in understanding the narrative that is to follow. I am going to recount that frightful history."

"And so the story begins with this little picture of Paris? It must be fascinating."

"You'll see. I married. My wife lived here with me. How I loved her! At first the feeling that my life would be short and I would scarcely be able to enjoy so much happiness assailed me; but I had not been married long when I became melancholy, and I started to brood...I am an inveterate brooder. I adored my wife and I was jealous of the very air she breathed."

"Now the matter's becoming really involved," I said to myself. "The marriage, the picture of Paris, the brooding love you felt for your wife...this is more confusing than the hall of antiquities."

And, in truth, I now regretted having provoked the doctor's tiresome account, in which I found nothing whatever of interest. Digressions, eccentricities—it all came down to that. I resigned myself, nonetheless, to listening.

"There were, in the early days of my marriage," he continued, "moments of indescribable happiness: I felt myself uplifted, spiritualized, mad; I felt a kind of cerebral inflammation and impulses to run, to shout, to talk to everyone. But suddenly I fell into the abyss of my cavillings, sinking in my own sadness. No one could make me utter a word. I had my idea, my torment, fixed in my mind. You don't know what it was?

"How should I know, for the love of heaven!"

"Oh!" he exclaimed, clenching his fists, his face flushed and a gleam of animation in his eyes. "It was because I thought....One day I entered my house late, I entered and I saw...."

The doctor stopped a moment, lost in thought, his head hidden in his hands, and remained silent a while.

This silence gave me a moment of respite and I looked around, where all was tranquility. A muffled growling broke the silence of the room: it was doña Monica, who was snoring, her head buried in her chest, free of cares, happy, giving free rein to her spirit, which was flying unrestrainedly who knows where. Her lips, shadowed by a slight moustache, stuck out in a snout, and through that and her flattened, fleshy nose, converted by the violence of her breathing into a true pipe organ, there issued the noisy symphony that was disturbing the profound silence of the laboratory. The doctor, raising his head again, continued:

"My wedding was a sudden affair: it was not preceded by those intimate, furtive relations that bind souls morally before the persons are bound by the religious and civil knot. I had not been her suitor; and it was something arranged by the parents, guided by convenience, rather than the spontaneous union of two lovers who have tired of the platonic life. We married not many days after having met; and I think that all my ills stemmed from that. I, nonetheless, loved her very much from the moment I resolved to marry her. But there came a day, and I don't know why, I thought I saw in her face signs of resignation rather than of joy, which grieved me beyond measure and made me consider; but when I began to suspect that I had proceeded incorrectly, I was already married. This did not prevent me from having some moments of happiness, as I said before; but they passed quickly, leaving me afterwards plunged in my thoughts. Do you know what the subject of my continual pondering was? I thought constantly about my wife, suspecting her fidelity in the future; this idea stuck in my mind so tenaciously that it gave me no rest. It occurred to me that I should be a tyrant with her, lock her in, avoid any occasion on which she might deceive me: sometimes my eyes locked with hers, and I tried to read her thoughts. The astonishment with which she viewed these quirks of mine, and so soon after our marriage, cannot be described: finally, she began to be afraid of me; and in good truth, I would have frightened anyone with my sinister austerity and introversion. She struggled to drive that idea from me; she appealed to reason; but reason sometimes seemed to me more insane than fantasy, and between the two of them they pushed me to the last stages of torment."

"But, you idiot, on what did you base that absurd suspicion?" I asked him, seeking to discover in Dr. Anselmo's musings a ray of logic.

"On nothing definite at that point. Later on you'll see. She was afraid of me; I knew it. But this is inexplicable, you can't understand it."

And, in effect, I understood nothing of all that gibberish, of those facts in which everything was confusion.

"You can't understand anything now, but you will afterwards, when I explain to you everything that happened to me. One day she was in that room I described to you just now; she was standing in front of that magnificent canvas of Paris and Helen of which I spoke to you. 'What a beautiful face!' she said, pointing at Paris. 'Yes,' I replied, looking at it as well. And the two of us gazed

18

for a while at the extraordinary beauty of that incomparable youth. Then she left, and I followed...."

"I understand less at every moment," I said to myself.

"What I have just recounted will explain in part my surprise, my terror, when one night I entered the house and saw...."

"But what?" I asked, wanting to know what the deluded doctor had seen.

"So that you can really understand this, I must acquaint you with the background of many things that greatly influenced the unheard of state of my spirit. I still remember her bedroom, illuminated by a mysterious light. I enter and I see her clothes strewn about in disorder, her jewels...I listen, and I hear the sound of her breath; I approach, with a tremulous hand I take the bed curtain, I lift it, I see her...I sense that I am near her bed...; her lips move, she seems about to speak...; she says nothing, nothing; but it seems to me that her lips have silently formed a word that does not reach my ear...; I draw closer...; it seems to me that she knits her eyebrows and then relaxes them...; I pay closer attention...; she seems to smile."

"All of this explains nothing," I observed, rather irritated upon seeing that nothing but drivel issued from the sage's mouth.

"All of this, my friend, is by way of explaining to you what must have been my stupor, my horror, when I saw...."

"What did you see, man? Let's have it," I said impatiently.

"I saw, I saw...."

The doctor was unable to go on, for a sudden, horrible noise, a tremendous detonation, resounded in the room, and an intense, reddish, infernal clarity illuminated us all. We gave a scream of terror. One of the retorts heating on the burner had burst with a deafening noise: the doctor, with his narrative, had forgotten the experiment, and the liquid, expanding considerably and finding no outlet, had forced its way out, igniting upon contact with the fire. There was a moment in which the place seemed a hell and everyone in it a demon. Doña Monica woke up terrified, screaming:

"Fire, fire!"

And she fainted at once, falling like a sack and flattening with her head the nearby guitar. The cat, who received a great part of the boiling liquid on his body, leapt from his place screaming in desperation: the poor thing mewed, ran with his fur afire, his eyes like flames, his whiskers burnt; he ran through the room with dizzying speed: he went up, down, jumped on top of the Christ, leaping from the feet to the head, from one arm to the other; he fell on a shell, slipped on the riding boots, tangled himself up in the coral branches, hopped on the skeleton, whose bones rang out frantically under the clawing; he fell to the floor again, threw himself on a stuffed bird, whose feathers flew for the first time after a century of quietude; the poor thing stretched, doubled over,

19

twisted, for his flesh crackled as though it were on a grill; he ran, he ran without stop, fleeing from himself and his own pains, and finally he dropped, swollen, sore, convulsed, thirsty, hair on end, rabid, in the midst of the room, where he kicked, mewed, clawed, lashed the floor with his tail and turned a thousand times in his slow, horrible agony.

CHAPTER II: THE OBSESSION

I

Finally and with great difficulty we put out the fire, keeping the flames from spreading and consuming us all. The only victim was the unhappy animal who, having received the boiling liquid on his skin, burned like a wick and perished, as we said, in frightful agony. A like lot befell a goodly portion of doña Monica's apron, where the flame had opened a large hole, after having burnt the lady's fingers when she tried to put it out. The scholar suffered no more serious misfortune than the total loss of a lock of hair that, with inveterate tenacity, more stubborn through time than through pomade, hung over his right temple. Finally the conflagration went out, and the old woman having stomped off in a fury because of the mischance, which she attributed to the "master's witchcraft," and heartsick at the sad end of the puss, whom she loved dearly, the doctor continued in this manner:

"I don't know on what I based my suspicions: I know that I had them. They entered me as innate ideas enter; or rather, they were in me, I believe, since I was born, who knows!, since the beginning, even before. I don't know what diabolical spirit it is that comes to whisper certain things in our ear when we are given over to thought; I don't know who concocts these arguments that enter our heads ready-made, firm, exact, with their infernal logic and their terrible evidence. One day I entered (listen well to this), I entered my house, dominated by those thoughts; as I drew near to Elena's room I thought I heard the voice of a man speaking very softly within; the voice stopped suddenly. They were aware of my approach....Afterwards I thought I heard hurrying footsteps, like someone fleeing, trying to make the least possible noise. I cannot tell you the sudden fury that took hold of me; I was blinded, I ran, I hurled myself at the door, I shoved it hard, I opened it at one blow, with such a crash that the walls shook with that intense convulsion of buildings when a storm strikes them or the ground in which they are cemented trembles."

"You must be terribly strong," I said ironically, noting how little resemblance there was between my unhappy friend and the sort of Samson we have pictured.

"Yes, the door opened, and Elena appeared in front of me, terrified, trembling, with such obvious signs of fear that I stopped, abashed in my turn. My first glance searched the room in a second. There was no man there; the window was not open; the interior door was also closed; it was impossible that in the instant that had elapsed between the sound of the voice and my entrance the locks could have been turned and the bolts thrown, nor had there been time enough for a person to leave by the door or jump through the window. I examined everything: I saw nothing. But I had heard that voice, I was sure of it, and I could not easily be convinced of the contrary either by the evidence of there being no one there, or by the heated protests of Elena, who in her hurt found words strong enough to reproach me and who called me a dreamer and a madman. She swore to me that she had been alone, that when I had entered in that manner she had thought she would die of fear, that she could not understand my conduct except through a complete alteration of my intellectual faculties."

"What strange ideas!" I said, considering what must have been the terror of that poor woman upon seeing her husband enter suddenly, furious and beside himself, swearing that he had heard a man's voice in her room.

"Strange, yes," replied the doctor, "but increasingly clearer and more vivid. I could not rid myself of my idea; the impression that voice had made on my ear was such that it still remains with me, and at that time, only by doubting my own existence, only by believing that I was not a real person, could I have accepted that as an illusion. It was nothing of the sort, and I was greatly strengthened in that belief when, on the following night...."

"Poor woman! What a night! You no doubt committed other atrocities of the same sort on the following night."

"Yes," he continued, "on the following night I beheld a phenomenon that took from me any hope of seeing clearly in that matter. What happened to me, my friend, exceeds the limits of the natural kingdom, and even today it is for me the confusion of all confusions. I entered my house, and I wandered a long time, alone and lost in thought, through those salons, where everything caused me displeasure and disgust: I passed through that room I have described, where the picture of Paris and Helen was located, and my blood ran cold with astonishment when I saw....It's the most stupendous phenomenon you can conceive of. The figure of Paris was not on the canvas. I thought I was mistaken, I went up to it, I touched the canvas, I lit a number of lights, I looked, I looked again....The figure of Paris—my God!—had disappeared; Helen was alone, and the expression on her face had changed completely, she being now sad and disconsolate who previously had appeared satisfied and happy. What infernal painting was this in which a figure could evaporate, be erased, go away as though it had body and life? I could not stop contemplating that accursed picture, and I said: 'But where is this devil of a man?' "

"Where was he? Drawn by an irresistible force, by my thoughts, by my jealousy, I ran to my wife's room. When I drew near, I detected the same voice as on the previous night, the same footsteps. I cannot describe my fury. 'I was right about that business last night,' I thought, and threw myself at the door. 'They've locked it!' I exclaimed, and beating heavily on it, or rather, throwing the entire weight of my body against it, I opened it, breaking it down. Upon entering I saw that the window that gave onto the garden was open, and that a shadow, an indistinct object, a man was jumping through it. It was so rapid that I scarcely saw him; I only saw his head in the moment of disappearing, his hands in the instant they released the window sill. I ran, I looked out, and I saw nothing; the night was extremely dark. I only thought I heard the thud of a body dropping. Elena looked at me, astonished, with an indescribable dread; she lost her senses, and this time she was unable to tell me that I was a dreamer and a madman, for she had lost the power of speech and fell at my feet like a dead woman. My only desire was to pursue that man until I found him, until I killed him. I went hastily down to the garden, and examined it with an anxiety impossible to describe: the walls were very tall, and no matter how dexterous and agile a man might be, he could not have jumped over them in the brief time it had taken me to come down. I examined everything: there was no one in the garden; but this garden opened onto a solitary patio with extremely high walls; I went there, and I had scarcely taken a step when I saw a shadow slipping cautiously through the mountains of stone that were there for the building of one of the pavilions of the palace. I lay in wait to see if, in effect, it was a man, or one of those images created by night and imagination, working in league. It was a man; I saw him go crouching along so as not to be discovered, and I don't know why it seemed to me that, in spite of the darkness of the night, I could distinguish in his face the features of that painted figure, whose disappearance from the picture caused me such uneasiness and confusion. The shadow, the man, or whatever it was, went slowly, ever cautiously, up to a well without curbstone, one of those that masons open during construction to have water closer at hand. To my amazement, he got slowly into the well; I saw his body lower itself little by little and disappear; then I saw nothing but the bust, then the head only; finally a hand, which continued to clutch the side. I remained for a while indecisive, watching attentively. A moment later he slowly, cautiously stuck out his head, as though to see if I were observing him, and immediately pulled it back rapidly. Finally the hand disappeared. I went up then, and a terrible revenge came to my imagination. As though my body were completely obedient to my unbridled passion, I felt my strength double and I acquired an extraordinary vigor; I picked up the biggest stone I could lift, I raised it with both hands to the level of my head, I jumped to the edge of the well and heaved it in, hurling it vigorously, for it

23

seemed to me that its own weight was not sufficient. Then I picked up a larger one, and I heaved it in with the same fury, not stopping until I had seized the third, for rage had doubled my strength. In ten minutes I hurled in more than fifty stones. This did not seem to me enough; I grabbed a nearby shovel and threw in dirt for the space of half an hour. I began to throw in stones again, and after two hours of unremittent work the well had disappeared and the ground was completely level. It still seemed very little to me, and I sat down on top of my work, exalted, trembling with fatigue, remaining there all night like the sentinel of my victory, turned into a cenotaph to watch over and cover that tomb. Sometimes it appeared to me that a Titan was lifting from below all the stones and earth I had thrown in. I should have liked to have been a statue of lead to weigh down eternally on my victim. Dawn came to shed some light on my mind. 'What have I done, my God?' I said, going inside and searching in the ordinary recourse of logic for the solution to that enigma; was he really a man or not?"

"One must confess, my friend," I said, unable to contain myself, "that if it was a man, you were a barbarian, and if it was a shadow, you were a fool."

"Don't judge me without knowing the rest," he continued. "When I went up, my first concern was to look at the picture of Paris again. The figure of the man was in its place. But I could not hold back a shudder of terror and icy cold when the painted face of the Trojan turned towards me, looked at me, and the damned man laughed with such a mocking expression that my hair stood on end."

"That's odd indeed," I said, "and exceeds in strangeness everything that went before."

"Is it not true, my friend, that this seems a most unlikely story?"

"I should say so! Quite unlikely!"

"That day," he went on, "consternation reigned in my wife's room. She was surrounded by her parents and those meddling relatives of the sort who are present at every critical moment, even when they haven't been called. She was crying, and the outraged Count Torbellino, her father, vowed that he had married his daughter to the most ferocious monster imaginable. Her mother, who was an old flirt, tried to console her, telling her to pay no mind to my odd starts and to take those attacks of frenzy that so tormented her calmly. When we were alone, Elena, at my feet, protested her innocence, adding that it was all my imagination, that no man had entered there, that no one jumped down from the balcony, that the door had been open—in short, so many things that I, persisting in my notion and sure of the reality of what I had seen, wavering in the most atrocious doubts, because her voice had a ring of total honesty, I thought I would go insane, and I was being driven inexorably to that state by this fatal, unheard-of situation."

"But my good man," I said to him, "was there no way of acquiring absolute certainty?"

24

"None, for everything worked against me, every day brought me new torture, the abnormal happenings being so numerous that they gave me no time to rest, to look for serenity and light. The events I have related to you are no more than the preparation or prologue to those I am now going to tell you, which is a thing unequaled in this life, for as far as I am aware no other human being has ever undergone such extraordinary and profound calamity. At some moments I was proud of myself, because I thought that with my decisive action I had put an end to that dismal incident. I considered it over and done; and when I thought of it in that way, not even the thought of having committed a great crime could reduce the pleasure that I took from it. But...listen to this, for this is the height of all that is marvelous. I was walking back and forth in my room, deep in thought as usual, when someone knocked lightly on the door: I was surprised that someone should have entered without being announced, and I said, 'Come in.' Imagine my surprise, my friend, when I saw—who do you think?—Paris himself entering my room, that very figure from the picture, but animate, alive; a man, in sum, a demigod with a frock coat, hat, gloves, and walking stick; a beautiful ideal converted into a modern-day gentleman, of the sort you see everywhere. His face was wicked and graceful, his smile ironic, his glance penetrating and lively, the same Paris, the very person from the canvas turned into a real being, a man of the nineteenth century. Consider my perturbation: I thought I was dreaming, I retreated in fright, I tried to call out, I thought of fleeing; but he, taking off his hat respectfully and making me a bow, finally convinced me that what I had in front of me was a real and tangible gentleman, whom for the time being I must treat as such, as befitted his considerable urbanity and fine matters."

II

"Do you know, my dear don Anselmo, that this has now passed the bounds of the marvelous?" I said to him. "But is it possible for the imagination, no matter how heated, to have sufficient force to give body to an idea in this manner?"

"I don't know, my friend," he replied. "I don't know what it was. I only know that I saw him as I'm seeing you now. He was beautiful, of an uncommon beauty, an amassment of all physical beauty the like of which I had never seen, if not in the works of ancient art. He dressed with a correct and serious elegance, like all those who have a true sense and exact notion of good grooming; he was, in sum, perfect in his face, in his body, in his clothing, in his manners, in everything."

"An extraordinary thing!" I exclaimed. "But didn't you touch him, didn't you try to ascertain if he were a dream, an apparition, one of those singular and incomprehensible optical phenomena that, when there is a fantasy ready to receive them, are produced by the reflection of the light?"

25

"I don't know what it was; what I can vouch for is that he had a real body, like yours, like mine, and a voice whose tone resembled no other."

"What, did he speak as well?" I said, astonished. "I thought he would leave after greeting you, as apparitions do."

"Leave! Nothing of the sort. You'll see. At first I didn't know what to do. I didn't know whether to call out or flee, fearing that nothing good could come of that visit; but finally I forced myself to be calm and after babbling a few words I motioned him to a seat. I resolved to speak clearly, and I said:

" 'May I know...?'

" 'Why I have come?' he answered. 'Yes, sir. I have come to do you a signal favor.'

" 'A favor?...Be so good as to explain yourself, for you have the advantage of me....I don't have the pleasure of your acquaintance.'

" 'Oh, yes, you know me, you met me not long ago,' he said with a malicious smile. 'Last night, without looking any further....'

" 'Last night!'

" 'Yes, last night. Don't you remember the rage with which you threw stones in a well, managing to fill it up at last?'

"These words and his smile froze my blood in my veins. He seemed unconcerned at my perturbation, and continued:

" 'I have come to speak with you for a purpose, to tell you that all those arms that you have tried to use against me are useless. You must know, sir, that I am immortal.'

"I cannot paint for you the perturbation that word produced in my soul: Immortal! 'But this man is the devil!' I said to myself, and I couldn't say a word, for I had a knot in my throat.

" 'Yes, sir, immortal,' he repeated calmly.

" 'And who are you?' I asked, making an effort.

" 'I am Paris.'

" 'Paris! I thought that was something out of mythology, or heroic history.'

" 'And so it is, in effect. But let us not go on forever now about my name and origin. I'm in a hurry, and I can't stay here long. The object of my visit is to tell you that you're tiring yourself out in vain in pursuing me. I can't be killed by knives or pistols or by being buried alive. Resign yourself, don Anselmo! It is all useless: there's nothing for it but to bow your head and suffer in silence. Someone up above has arranged that things should be this way.'

" 'Sir,' I said, in a fever of anxiety and trying to take charge in that most peculiar situation, 'I warn you that I cannot tolerate jokes of this sort. Have the goodness to leave.'

" 'Gently, gently, my dear sir. You have a bad temper. You are insufferable. That's why you fill poor Elena with such horror.'

" 'How dare you speak her name?'

" 'Why not? After all, she loves me!' he exclaimed, smiling.

" 'Monster!' I shouted, rising furiously and threatening him, 'be silent, or here and now....'

"Be careful!" I said in my turn, taking a step backwards upon seeing that don Anselmo, recounting that passage, stood up and started towards me with his fists closed, as though I were the infernal apparition who had so tormented him.

"Remembering all that," the doctor went on, more calmly, "I become so annoyed I cannot control myself. When I threatened him, he stayed cool as you please. He smiled and looked at me with that disdainful and somewhat mocking compassion that the words and deeds of madmen inspire. His serenity made me despair the more, his smile killed me; I don't know what I would have given to be able to strangle him. Afterwards, as though my anger were no more than the tantrum of a child, Paris continued:

" 'She loves me. We love one another, we complement each other, we are drawn together by a fatal law. You ask me who I am: I'm going to see if I can make you understand it. I am what you fear, what you think. I am that fixed idea that you have in your mind. I am that intimate pain, that inexplicable uneasiness. But I have existed since the beginning of the world. My age is that of humankind, and I have travelled through all the countries of the world where men have instituted a society, a family, a tribe. In some places they've called me *Demon of wedded bliss;* but I have always scorned this nickname and others like it, and I have resolved to carry no set name; thus it is that I am called Paris, Aegisthus, Norris, Paolo, Buckingham, or Beltran de la Cueva, according to the country I am in and the persons with whom I am dealing. As to my influence on the lofty destinies of Humanity, I will say that I have touched off heinous wars, giving rise to the greatest public and domestic disasters. In every religion there is some edict or other against me, especially in yours, which devotes to me the whole of the last commandment. Moralists have dared to defy me, and philosophers have had the bad taste to publish impertinent libels against my humble person, some of them even allowing themselves to try to root me out completely, imbeciles!, as though I were a corn or an abscess. They have tried to finish me off, as though I could perish, as though immortality were subject to the action of the mortal weapons at their disposal. Thus it is that because of honor and self-esteem I find myself obliged to continue playing my role of scourge with all the diligence and recourses my double nature is capable of. Here you see me always active, always effective; the large centers of population are my preferred abode, for you must know that the countryside, villages, hamlets, are repugnant to me, and only occasionally do I bother to visit them out of pure curiosity. It's in the capitals that I like to live. Oh! I have always loved these places, where comfort, refined culture, and elegant idleness offer me their invincible arms and their so efficacious weapons. I like splendor and voluptuousness: I am as sybaritic as my old friend Semiramis, to whom I gave immortality. Believe me, my friend, Babylon was worth more than these deities you are all so vain of; yes, it was worth more. And as to clothing, I prefer the light gauzes of olden times, and it bothers me to have to give in to the exigencies of modern prudery, an evil being I have been able to corrupt only partially in matters of dress. As to the rest, I don't do too badly; moralists condemn me and would-be philosophers treat me as though I were a sophist evil; but that matters very little to me. Those who are insufficiently stupid, who aren't so bereft of their senses as to be philosphers, applaud me, imitate me, point me out when they see me. Women are my most sincere friends, although some of them treat me with a certain amount of mistrust, the result of the slanders of sages rather than of my own character. Others show me considerable graciousness, and some of them talk to me of their husbands in a way that makes me laugh. That's the sum of my literature. On the other hand, I'm not ambitious; I'm one of those who is satisfied with the grass on my own side of the fence, and I detest marital anarchy, always trying to put it down, in company with some domestic moralists, who know how not to provoke that anarchy, by cultivating my friendship, which is always disinterested. I don't like scandal, and I always practice the most silent means of arriving at an end that is more silent yet; I have abandoned the old, discredited means of scaling walls, surprises, bribes, so as to distinguish myself from a certain counterfeit image of me that walks the world, a so-called Don Juan, who is an insolent usurper, and, besides, a scourge not greatly to be feared. So, my friend, not to be afraid and we'll finish up quickly. Understand that it's written, as the Muslims would say. I am like death: the hour strikes and I come. It is as impossible to avoid me as it is to avoid my confrere.'

"When I heard this speech, I resolved to make an effort to see if I could decipher the frightful enigma. Pretending a serenity I did not have, and taking the matter with the proper calm that seemed appropriate to me, I stood up and said:

" 'Sir, I must inform you that I am not disposed to tolerate your improprieties. You must know that I am old enough not to believe in witchcraft, nor have I the patience necessary to suffer your lunacies.'

" 'This man is determined not to understand me. Are you aware that Elena is mine?' he said, after laughing uproariously, with the easy expression that comes from a resolve not to allow oneself to become upset for anything.

" 'Don't say that name again,' I shouted, unable to control my anger.

" 'But I've come precisely for her...,' said Paris in a wicked tone of voice that made my hair stand on end.

" 'Scoundrel! What are you saying? For her!' I exclaimed violently.

" 'Yes, for her. We agreed on it last night, and....'

" 'Last night? Oh, I am mad! Demon, infernal man, or whatever you may be, explain this dark riddle to me. I can't live this way: I want to know what all this is...But Elena is innocent. She's sworn to me that she's never seen you.'

" 'Oh, but she has seen me.'

" 'When?'

" 'Always, at every hour. But you don't understand these things: I'm going to explain it to you clearly.' "

III

Don Anselmo rested for a while, for the preceding narrative, with its intermittent dialogue, had tired him considerably. When he had calmed down for a moment, trying to quieten the agitation that was devouring him, he continued his story in the following manner:

" 'The shadow, the demon, the demigod, the picture, or whatever it was, looked at me a while with that malicious smile that had been so well portrayed by the artist in the picture where he had previously been, and then said to me:

" 'Oh yes, she's seen me. She sees me everywhere. When she said that *yes*, that vow of which her husband is so proud, she saw me in the altar, in the lights, in the white material of her dress, in the black stuff of your dress coat. From that moment on, she has found me everywhere, in every reflection she finds the light of my glance, in every echo she hears my voice, in her own shadow she sees mine....She opens her prayer book, and the letters move around to form my name. She speaks with God, and without meaning to, she speaks with me. She thinks she hears the noise of the air, the deep, constant sound of Nature, and she hears my words. She's awake, and she waits for me. She's alone, and she remembers me. She's asleep, and she invokes me. Her imagination flies restlessly in search of me, never ceasing. I live in her consciousness, where I am forever weaving an endless cloth. I live in her mind, where I have lit a flame that I feed constantly. Her feelings, her ideas, I am all that. So you may judge whether or not I have cause to say she has seen me.'

" 'Infernal spirit!' I shouted, dizzy and rather fascinated, 'I don't understand a word of this gibberish. Didn't you say that you've come for her?'

" 'Yes.'

" 'Scoundrel! Leave my house this instant,' I exclaimed, trying to shake off my bewilderment.

" 'I won't go without her.'

" 'Fiend! Didn't you say that the age of abductions is past?'

" 'I'll explain myself: what I want to take away is not the person of Elena; what I want to take is your wife.'

" 'Sophist, mischiefmaker, and what difference do you find between my wife and the person of Elena?'

" 'A great deal, my dear don Anselmo,' he replied.

"He made me a subtle, labyrinthine speech that left my poor head in a more confused state than ever. I am forced to confess that his voice fascinated me, and that it seemed to me very different from all the voices we are used to hearing. And if I were to say that in the midst of the fear, the upheaval that I felt, that his explanations caused me a sort of amazement not unakin to pleasure, I would most certainly not be lying."

"I confess, don Anselmo," I said, "that I have never heard anything to resemble this singular case of yours. The apparition who introduces himself in that manner, his language, the familiarity with which he speaks, it all seems so absurd to me that, if it were not you telling it, I should judge it to be pure invention, the work of hack writers and others who are enemy to the truth."

"Well, it's as sure that I saw him and spoke to him and that he said to me what I've related, as it is sure that you and I exist and are here talking."

"In good truth, it's unheard of," I pointed out, "that imagination, with no external influence, should be able to give life and body to beings like that devil Paris who introduced himself to you so inopportunely. There's no doubt that that gentleman was nothing other than the personification of an idea, of that constant, tenacious idea that, for some time past, and especially since your wedding, you'd had lodged in your brain. What I cannot explain to myself is how that idea acquired material and corporal existence; nor do I know to what class of spontaneous generation that phenomenon, unprecedented in the history of hallucinations, is due. But go on, let's see where all this is leading."

"What he said to me has remained indelibly engraved in my memory," continued the doctor, heaving a sigh. "Nothing is as vivid to me as what he answered me when I asked him what difference there was for him between the person of Elena and my wife. He spoke thus:

" 'I don't want the person of your good lady. The wife, my friend, the wife is what I'm looking for; I want to take over half your bed and show it to the entire world. That doesn't mean that I want to destroy the institution: I respect the sacrament; but I intend to take away something that exceeds the institution in value, and is above the sacrament.... Three powers establish matrimony: the civil, the ecclesiastical, and another that is in the hands of neither the vicars nor the curates, but is controlled rather by what we call the masses, society, people, the public, riffraff, neighbors, friends, in short, the world. You already know that the world breaks certain ties that appear unbreakable. Very well: I want to carry away from here what the world needs in order to break those ties; I want to carry the husband's abdication of his personality, the acknowledgement of his weakness. Thus I will feed the masses, the people who live from this. Everyone will ask me about you and about her; but my very presence is a definitive reply, for I am by my very nature the negation of the tie that unites you. I want to take outside the love that she professes for me, to make public what today exists only in her imagination, a bad thought, what today is only in your brain, a suspicion. I want to make of your doubts, of your jealousy, of your imaginings, of your follies, of your desires, of your insane illusions, a great book that will pass from hand to hand and that will be read and reread eagerly. I want to take away with me the pains that you suffer, the repugnance and horror you inspire in her. Keep her person: I have no desire for it. What I will take and show in the public square is: the look she directs at me, the rendezvous she makes with me, the favors she grants me, the rebuffs she gives you, the reticence she reveals when speaking of you, the epithet of *good* that she'll apply to you from time to time. What I will take away is the opinion of your maid, of your groom, who will be ready to tell a tale for money; I will take away the key to your convenient absentmindedness and my timely visits. Keep your wife: I will do nothing more than stroll back and forth in front of her and everyone, receive her tender looks in the presence of hundreds of persons, sprinkle her favorite perfume on my body, walk up and down the streets so that it will always look as though I'm just coming from here, and in the darkness of the night throw my shadow on the walls of your garden. That is what I want.'

"When I heard this, my friend, my rage was so great that I made a move to strike him; and I would have done, had not a secret force, a sort of respectful terror held me back."

"I see that that Paris, who presented himself so courteously in your house, in the end was treating you with irreverent familiarity," I said to him. "I have noticed that at the last he was speaking to you as though to a servant, or an inferior."

"Yes, that scoundrel, shortly after beginning to speak with me, left off all dissembling. He lounged back at his ease in the chair, he addressed me contemptuously, at times he strolled through the room with his hands in his pockets, and finally he took out a cigar and began to smoke with the greatest casualness."

"But, man," I said to him, "why didn't you try to see if the shadow wouldn't have vanished with a blow or two?"

"Consider what I did. My situation was so terrible, that I resolved to act energetically. 'I have got to put a stop to this,' I thought, and, planting myself in front of him, I said to him:

" 'Sir, this is a tissue of lies, and you are an imposter come here to make fun of me. Do you think I believe these idiotic statements that you've made about your double nature, and about your being immortal? I'm not a madman that I should believe all that. I'm going to break your skull this very day, do you hear me?'

" 'You want to fight with me?' he said, with mocking familiarity. 'Very well, we'll fight, which is to say, I'll kill you.'

" Oh! I'll fight with a legion like you,' I shouted at the height of my wrath. 'I'll kill you, I'll cut off your head with more pleasure than if I were to destroy a tiger, a boa.'

" 'I stand by what I said before.'

" 'I'd kill you,' I continued with redoubled fury, 'were all the powers of hell to protect you. I don't know how to use any weapon, but God will come to my aid. You say that you've come to take away my honor. Well, I will prevail against you, you fiend of all times, you perverse genius of all lands. It's useless for you to try to disarm me with your cruel irony, to frighten me with the tale of what you are and what you can do. If you're a man, I'll kill you. I'm sure of it. If you're a spirit, I'll annihilate you just the same, for God will come to my assistance. He will make me his instrument to extirpate such a monstrosity and aberration.'

" 'Very well,' replied Paris, tossing away the stub of his cigar. 'We'll fight tonight.'

" 'Why tonight? Today, right now.'

"Hatred had made me eloquent. As to my determination to fight with that supernatural being, it can be explained by the state of my spirit. Death held no fear for me. On the contrary, it struck me as a relief. If he killed me, all my troubles were over. If he was a man, I might be lucky enough to finish him off. If he was a spirit..., in short, of what use is it to reason at such a moment? My decision was made, and I wouldn't have changed it for anything."

"But my good man," I said to him, "wasn't it reckless to take that step, to risk death?"

"I don't know what it was. I wanted to put an end to it," responded the doctor, "and I saw no other way of clearing up the mystery."

"And did you fight?"

"Yes. I didn't want seconds. I wanted that duel to be as solitary as my grief. Dying mattered to me not at all. Determined not to prolong my agony, we went that very afternoon to a place near the capital."

"But without witnesses!"

"We took two pistols. We both went in my carriage and his good humor was so marked along the way that I was even more convinced of the certain imminence of my death. For me, that business was in reality a suicide that I was carrying out in an unusual and new form."

"And what was the outcome? I'm curious to know how you behaved in front of so dreadful an adversary."

"Oh, my friend!" said the doctor, "the outcome is the oddest part of the adventure, and you cannot possibly guess it. I assure you that it is completely different from what you have imagined."

IV

I confess that Dr. Anselmo's narrative was beginning to interest me a bit, only out of curiosity, of course, for there was nothing in it that was likely or realistic.

There was, nonetheless, a small amount of sense at the bottom of all that nonsense, for the figure of Paris, an imaginary being to whom my friend's great fantasy had given apparent existence, could very well pass for one of society's major voices. If the doctor invented all that, one must admit that his invention was not without a certain suspense. If, on the other hand, he thought what he was relating was true, he was one of the greatest visionaries ever to have been seen. Anxious to know how that extraordinary duel had turned out, I urged him to go on. He didn't have to be asked twice.

"Paris and I went in my carriage to the place we had selected. We spoke very little along the way, although he tried to start up a conversation, digging at me with barbed comments and witticisms that I don't want to remember. I could only think of death, which I thought was near, and which inspired me with more joy than sorrow. My serenity was not the serenity of courage, but of resignation. At that moment the world, my riches, my wife, all bored and repelled me. I saw the end of all my troubles close at hand, and that man, that diabolical man in human form, seemed more my salvation than my enemy.

"When we reached the site of the duel, evening was falling and the West was lit up with splendid colors and reflections. The air was cool and humid, and so gentle that the leaves, yellow and weak from autumn's cold, scarcely moved. Without having to be shaken, they fell from their own weight, dead and livid before they left the tree. I-remember that afternoon as though it were yesterday. The coach stopped, we got down and walked a good stretch alone."

"My dear don Anselmo!" I exclaimed, "you must admit that the procedures of that duel are of the most incomprehensible unlikelihood. To go out to kill each other without witnesses, to take your opponent up in your own carriage!... That wouldn't happen anywhere, and I'm sure this is the first example of it to be seen in modern society."

"Unlikelihood!" exclaimed don Anselmo, "who can talk of that when dealing with a case that is outside the limits of the human? Don't look for order in this. If this were the sort of thing that happens ordinarily, I wouldn't relate it."

This argument did not lack force, and I fell silent.

"When we had selected the place, Paris said to me:

" 'The pistols?'

" 'They're good,' I replied, handing them to him.

" 'It's all the same to me,' he answered without examining them. 'All weapons work for me. Load them in front of me, and then we'll draw lots to see who shoots first.'

" 'They're already loaded.'

" 'Let's see how we can draw lots,' said Paris, strolling through the field with the same naturalness and ease with which he had strolled through my room.

" 'With a handkerchief,' I said. 'We can make a knot in one of the corners and the one who....'

" 'It seems to me you're a bit of a sharper,' suggested Paris, laughing with all the aplomb of someone who knows he's going to kill his man.

" 'Let's throw a coin on the ground,' I added impatiently, for those preparations to arrive at an end that to me was unquestionable bothered me.

" 'Very well. Heads, I shoot.'

" 'And tails, I go first.'

" 'Go on, toss the coin and have done.'

"I pitched the coin, it fell to the ground, and we both bent over to make it out. It was tails: I was to shoot first. We positioned ourselves at ten paces. I aimed, or at least I raised my arm, trying to direct the barrel of the pistol towards my enemy's chest. He laughed when he saw the barrel of the weapon describing such curves in the air, and addressed a number of witty comments to me that disconcerted me even more, obliging me to lower my hand, for, my fingers having grown cold from the afternoon air, I didn't even have sufficient force to pull the trigger. But I immediately aimed again, so as not to go to the next world without having played for good or ill the role that honor had assigned me in that critical occasion. I held it out without trying to aim and closed my eyes. The shot rang out, and Paris fell to the ground without a cry, for the shot had gone straight through his chest."

"The devil you say!" I exclaimed upon hearing the unexpected outcome of the dispute. "He died?"

"The contemplation of a miracle," continued the doctor, "would not have caused me such astonishment as that victory acquired over such a terrible adversary. To kill such a man, to win out over such an evil genius, was more than could be hoped for from one who had never wielded a weapon nor learned to fight with antagonists from the other world. I had vanquished the greatest enemy of marital peace. If he was a man, I had freed the world of a fiend. If he was the personification of a vice, a human scourge, a social calamity incarnate in an arrogant body, then I had ridded society of the half of its scandals. I thought that some heavenly divinity had come to my assistance. 'Oh! My honor,' I thought, 'my honor, this pure, clean emotion, has been for me the protective divinity that has guided my arm. It has breathed a breath of life into this ball, so that it could fly, aware and angry, to that chest to split open that heart, center of perfidy and deceit. My God! If duelling is a crime, if what I have just done is a murder, forgive this fault, the forerunner of innumerable benefits. You, who have permitted the presence of this monster, you, who are the master and wise dispenser of rewards and punishments, you, who give the beneficial rain, the dew, the sun, manna, and who permit plague, hunger, and fire, you will forgive, you will forgive the sacrifice of this being you created for our punishment, imposing on us the task of conquering him.'

"I examined the body of Paris carefully, and I saw that a river of blood was gushing from his wound, but he was still alive. He was breathing, he moved his

34

eyes slowly and looked at me with an expression I couldn't make out very well.

"His look was not one of sadness or pain. The queer state of my head caused me to see a mocking smile on his lips. But in spite of that, his face was livid, and his body faint and limp. Can you believe that when I saw him so I was sorry for him, and that there was a moment in which my anger dissipated? In the final analysis, we're men. Besides, when I touched him, when I made certain through my own senses that that was a human body, the belief that he was a shadow, the creation of my imagination, disappeared from my thoughts. At that moment I only thought that he was a young man who, having guessed my thoughts, had tried to play a joke on me or make fun of me, passing himself off in my eyes as a supernatural being. In short, when I saw that man, wounded by me, bleeding on a lonely field, with the help of no one, without bodily or spiritual comfort to soften somewhat his now certain death, I felt such pity for him that I resolved to put him in the carriage and take him to my house to give him the help he needed."

"But didn't you understand,' I queried him, 'that you were leaving yourself open to discovery?"

"I would have abandoned him had he been dead. But he was alive, he was breathing. How could I leave him there? My sensibility could not contemplate such an act. Besides, my hatred had disappeared in the face of victory. I did not waver in my resolution; I put him in the carriage with the help of my servants, and...so, home."

"But couldn't you have left him somewhere else?"

"No. In my house they wouldn't discover him, because I would take every conceivable precaution. Abandoned or turned over to someone else, he would indeed be discovered immediately. That was my line of reasoning on the way home. We arrived when night was far advanced. No one saw us enter; we carried him up very carefully and put him in a bed. When I was alone with him, I examined him closely. He was still alive. I was greatly surprised that, far from being feebler, weaker, nearer to death from his grave wound, he appeared more animated, and fixed his serene, observant gaze on the objects that decorated the room. When he felt me near, he stared at me with a tenacity that made me tremble. He seemed to fathom the very depths of my soul. Those were not the eyes of a dying man. After looking at me a long time without blinking, his hand, cold as marble, touched my hand, communicating to me a glacial current that circulated through my body, causing me to shiver with an emotion I had never known. His lips moved as though to utter a groan, and a voice, that seemed to come not out of his mouth but from some invisible depth, a voice of immense resonance and gravity, pronounced these words, that I cannot remember without dread:

" 'Fool, I am immortal.'

"It still seems to me as though I'm looking at him, listening to him," went on the doctor somewhat absently.

Afterwards he began to gaze attentively at the ceiling, as though there were something written up there. Lost in his musings, his eyes went to the sky, taking on that attitude of a saint that was peculiar to him. Then he continued the story as follows:

"I don't know what I thought then. It occurred to me to shut him up there and wait days, weeks, months, to see if that cursed being could exist wounded, alone, without food or drink. Meanwhile, blood flowed from his wound, without his body becoming any weaker because of this. On the contrary, he grew livelier and livelier, adding to my despair. You shall say if it wasn't enough to drive one mad. To be constantly pursued by that demon, who hadn't been able to kill me either, and who had finally installed himself in my house, next to me, like my conscience, like my thoughts, like my fear! My rage knew no bounds when I saw him sit up in the bed and exclaim:

" 'Now you see how I have managed not to leave your house. Will you dare to turn out of your house a man whom you have wounded, a man who is bleeding and dying? If you throw me out, it's impossible for you to escape being branded a murderer. It will be discovered that you have tried to kill a man, the police will come, there will be a scandal....They'll say that the good don Anselmo found a lover in his wife's room and shot him. You see what a scandal there'll be! If you want me to go away, I'll go away; but I told you very clearly that when I left this house I would take your honor with me. Dolt, in vain do you try to prevail against me, against that which is immortal, omnipotent, divine. I am superior to men; I am part of that evil which since the beginning has weighed on your existence, and from which you cannot free yourselves, for a supreme law has imposed it on you and yours as a part of life. Here I am, in your house; that is what I wanted. Elena knows that I'm here. A number of outsiders know it, too. But for now it's a secret kept by many. If you want there to be a scandal, if you want a thousand voices to talk of me, if you want this bandied about in the streets and squares, throw me out of here. I'll go happily, but you know everything that I'll take with me.'

" 'But what forces can be used against you?' I exclaimed, at the peak of my confusion. 'Whether moral or material, there must be some forces that can conquer you, you incomprehensible demon, more fatal than all the demons that are used to tempt man, carrying him along through the pathways of all the vices.'

" 'Against me, nothing can prevail,' he answered, recovering little by little his habitual good humor and levity. 'No weapon can wound me. Don't take what has happened seriously. Don't think that you have won out over me, you poor madman. What you have seen was nothing more than an incident prepared with the object of trapping you the better. This house is mine now. I've penetrated it and you can't turn me out. Everyone knows that Paris has entered your house, and you, though you were to employ all your faculties, all your money, everything that exists and is of any value on the face of the earth, you would not be able to convince anyone of the contrary....'

" 'Oh! I don't know what I'll do!' I shouted despairingly. 'I'm going to set fire to this house so that we'll all perish.'

" 'Fire!' he said, laughing diabolically and sitting up in the bed, 'Fire! But that is my food, I live on it; fire is my blood, my breath, my look, my word; I burn, I devour, I annihilate. Don't set up against my power those venal elements that at a sign from me obey submissively. I tell the air: "Ruffle her hair, carry echoes to her ear that will plunge her in those vague musings from whose confusion emerges luminously, inexorably, the first wicked thought." And the air obeys me. I tell the water: "Go and caress her body, indolently abandoned in the waves of her bath, with stimulating cold or soft warmth; spread languor through that body and upset the serenity of her mind, producing that voluptuous giddiness that deceives the conscience and makes accessible the fortress of modesty." And the water obeys me. I tell the fire: "Run through her veins, kindle her heart with passion, make that inflaming spark that is the final abdication of will burst forth in her thoughts." And the fire obeys me. I tell the light: "Reflect the beautiful line of her face in the mirror, and carry the image of her neck, her lip, her hair, her figure, from her mirror to her eyes, so that her self-love, the formidable bulwark that defends me, may grow." And the light obeys me. More than that: I *am* that murmuring air, that voluptuous water, that fire that inflames, that light that flatters. You're blind: you are looking at me, you think that I'm here. No, I'm there, next to her; I never abandon her, because I am her idea, her wicked thought, her wicked desire: I never leave her side. In vain do you try to pursue that wicked thought, that desire, when, through a singular phenomenon, it presents itself to you in human form. Dullard, don't you understand that I can't be buried under a mountain of stones? Don't you see that it's impossible to kill me with a shot as you would kill a bird, a thief?'

" 'Be silent, for pity's sake, you monster!' I exclaimed in distress. 'What crime have I committed to warrant such a great torment? For this is a punishment, yes, for some crime of which I am in ignorance. I, who am integrity itself, honor, loyalty, sobriety, why have I deserved this torture, which upsets all my faculties and will end by driving me insane?'

" 'It's your own fault,' said Paris serenely, showing no signs now of weakness, as though a supernatural physician had cured his wound through enchantment. 'It's your fault, you, who called me, who brought me, who evoked me with the force of your mind and fantasy.'

" 'Well I, with that same force, conjure you to leave me in peace. I can't live this way, you devil, spirit, thought, or whatever you may be. Go; I banish you from my head; I expel you from me, since you refuse to kill me; go, because this is a thousand times worse than dying.'

" I, go! That cannot be,' replied my enemy, lighting a cigarette. 'I haven't the power to leave you, even if I wanted to do so. So long as you have ideas and feelings, I shall be here. Renounce all that and I will leave; resign yourself to being, instead of an intelligent, sensitive man, an automatic machine, with no spiritual life; resign yourself to being a living object, a thing, and then I'll go.'

" 'I'll resign myself. I want to die and not think; I want to be a beast and not feel in my head this thing that I have carried from the moment of birth, for my torment.'

" 'Don't take it so to heart,' he replied. 'These things should be considered calmly; be philosophical; have that great serenity that has made so many husbands famous, and don't try to impose a false sense of honor on certain social laws no one can go against.'

" 'Don't upset me any further; I want to die; I want to be sacrificed to that thought that has devoured me, consuming me entirely.' "

"I said all that in utmost sincerity, my friend; I wanted to die, or to live without consciousness or understanding, if this was living; there was a sort of delirium in me, such an excitement that I have never since experienced anything of the sort. I stared at that man, I touched him, I was seeing him, I had all the necessary grounds for believing in his existence, and still it all seemed a dream to me.

"Has it never happened to you that upon suffering the torments of a nightmare, you are completely unbelieving in the face of so much pain, and you say: 'This is a dream,' as though a spark of reason were on the watch when all your faculties were clouded over, except fantasy, which dominates everything at will? Well, the same did I, in that anguished delirium, say to myself at times: 'This is a dream.' But reality gave me the lie: I was in my house; I recognized myself to be awake, as I recognize myself to be alive now. I came and went, captive to a horrible anxiety, and everything that surrounded me was real: the people were the same; the objects, identical. I left my room to see if the effect of external things might give me some light; but I accomplished nothing. Finally, I determined to leave there: I locked the room, leaving the wounded man inside, and went to Elena's room. When I entered, my wife drew back in fear, trembled, and then babbled a few words at me, for she had lost her voice from terror. I don't know what intimate conviction made me look at everything, examine everything, agitated, convulsed, demented. The unhappy woman moaned: I believe I abused her. Afterwards, going from one spot to another, I examined everything intensely, and such was my upheaval, that I even tried to find what I was looking for under the chairs, in the vases on her dressing table, and among the leaves of her books. There was nothing there; I saw nothing; but I had the deep conviction that he was there: in the air, in the shadow, in the perfume, in the echo of our voices, in everything I seemed to sense the presence of that depraved being. 'Where is he?' I shouted; 'there's someone here!' 'Who?' she said, desperate. 'Him,' I answered, 'that monster, that spirit of a man. I know that he's here, I feel him, I hear him. Yes, Elena, he's here; you have him. I see him in your eyes, I hear him in your voice; he's here.'

"And, in effect, the shadow of all the objects seemed to me his shadow, the echo of our voices seemed to me his voice, and in the vague accidents of light, sound, touch, I seemed to find something of the person, of the breath of that execrable genius. Elena wept so mournfully that it was impossible to recriminate with her. I only said to her: 'Yes, he's here, he's here.' Finally I left, for I was becoming more and more upset, and I returned to my room, where I had left him locked in. Upon entering, I uttered a cry: the wounded man was not there. My terror was such that I was unable to take a step, and I dropped into a chair. I had no forces left because of the continual and painful impressions of that day; I swooned, I fainted, and had not my nature given way spontaneously to sleep, I don't know what would have become of me. I remained motionless and as though dead for many hours. When I came to my senses, it was dawning. I heard a noise at the door, I looked, and it was Paris who was entering in a dressing gown, slippers, his hair in disorder, like someone just getting out of bed. He passed in front of me, looking at me with that diabolical smile characteristic of him. I looked at him a long time too, and the stupor, and a certain emotional lethargy that I felt, prevented me from speaking to him for a long time."

While he was relating this, the doctor was again experiencing that emotional lethargy of which he was speaking. His eyes were glazed, his voice slow, his breath labored, he was tired, and no doubt the remembrance of the events under discussion produced in him a very strong emotion. For that reason, and considering what the poor man was suffering by calling to mind his insane idea, I did not dare make him the thousand observations that occurred to me concerning the case, reflections that would have dampened considerably the enthusiasm and faith with which he related such lunacies.

CHAPTER III: ALEJANDRO

I

That night the doctor was unable to continue his curious story, which, by sheer virtue of extravagance, had interested me somewhat. I wanted to know what would be the final act of the mischievous hero of antiquity who had determined to take away my poor friend's judgement, if indeed he had any. It was quite obvious that it would have to end soon in one fashion or another, for it wasn't possible for such an invention, or whatever it was, to last longer than the law of art demands, and besides, by the last things my friend had related, one could see that the dénouement couldn't be far off. But that night, as I've said, he was unable to satisfy my desire: he would have done so, in spite of his tiredness and the emotional state in which he found himself as a result of the recollection of his misfortunes; but I didn't urge him to go on, and we agreed to hold another session on the following night, which we did. Picking up the interrupted thread of his discourse, he continued thusly:

"Where did we leave off? Because from last night to now I've forgotten; and whenever I remember that affair there is a derangement in my faculties, which are never in the best of shape."

"We stopped with an extremely interesting incident. You had fainted, you'd gone to sleep, surrendering to a deep sleep, which for my part I consider to have been the work of some spell by that infernal being, and when you awoke, near day, you saw Paris appear, in a dressing gown and slippers, as though he had just gotten out of bed."

"You're right, that was it," he said, "and I, as I indicated to you, in my stupor was unable to say a word to him for some time; I looked at him, feeling something of that giddiness that precedes a profound lethargy; I watched him stroll through the room with his hands in the pockets of the dressing gown, take out a cigar, strike a match, scratching it against the box, and then begin smoking as coolly as you please."

"And the two of you didn't speak?"

"Oh yes, we spoke. The strange thing is that that dressing gown was mine, and it fitted him to the inch, as though it had been tailor-made for him."

"It's obvious that that charlatan wanted to take over everything that belonged to you," I observed; and I repented shortly after of having made such an observation.

"Yes," he said sadly. "Finally, seeing that I could do nothing against that miserable being; seeing that I couldn't conquer him, that I couldn't kill him, that I couldn't throw him out of my house, I resolved to surrender to the pain, to give up, incapable of resisting any longer. I didn't insult Paris, I didn't curse him, I didn't try to harm him, for nothing worked against him. I laid aside my ire, exchanging it for a serene resignation, which was of some relief to me at that time.

" 'I'm going,' I told him, 'since I can't do anything against you. You invulnerable demon, I leave you everything: my house, my riches, my position, my wife; it's all in your hands, including my honor, which I have not been able to wrest from you. I am speaking of my honor in the opinion of others, for my honor in my own consciousness will always go with me, and you can't take it from me with your evil arts. I prefer to wander far from here, in some unknown country, despised by all, rather than bear this torment in which I live, deprived of the most innocent pleasures of my home. I want to flee; stay here, in full possession; I consider myself defeated.'

" 'Fool!' he replied, looking at me. 'Where are you to go that I cannot follow you? Remember what I told you last night. If when you go you leave here your understanding and fantasy, what there is in you of the divine, what distinguishes you from the beasts, you may leave tranquilly, I won't bother you; but if not, don't cry victory, for I'll go with you in this or some other form; when I become fond of a person I don't desert him easily.'

" 'But if I'm leaving you everything,' I replied, 'what more do you want? I no longer fear dishonor, I don't fear scandal, I don't fear anything. You can enjoy your handiwork; it doesn't matter to me if they talk about me, if they point at me, if they insult me with the most vilifying nicknames. What more do you want of me?'

" 'Calm yourself, Anselmo!' exclaimed Paris. 'Where would you go alone, wandering through those lands, pursued always by me, even though in a different form? Be calm; reflect, consider the gravity of your decision. Don't you see that this is a cowardly act unworthy of a brave man? Accept the martyrdom, and withstand it to the end, as befits someone with pretensions to a superior spirit and to that integrity which ennobles men more than frantic and reckless foolhardiness. Here is where you should always be, in the presence of your grief, always in your place, bearing one after another the anguishes of this crisis, which is nothing new in the world and has overset many a one before now. Here, my friend, here. You can't say that I'm not conscientious, that I don't reason with the maturity that distinguishes serious persons from feather-headed and presumptuous beardless youths.'

" 'Oh, this is too much!' I said. 'Am I not to leave here, not to leave this house? Are you also to pursue me far from these places? This can't be; and if by chance it is so, I will become a brute, I will cease thinking, as you've said; I will be the dullest and most bestial of animals. If this is what it is to be a man, I curse my condition, and I laugh at this pompous bombast with which some seek to ennoble it, saying that we are the kings of creation. What imbecility!'

" 'Yes, that is what it is to be a man!' he affirmed, 'and that is what it is to be king of creation. I have lived from the beginning of the world, and I have been present at a multitude of terrible happenings, individual and social. I know what sorrows are, whose importance is such in the sphere of life that some have gone beyond the limits of the personal to stir the emotions of the world, as happened in the war of Troy, whose details I remember as though they had taken place yesterday. From what I have seen since then, I understand that the person is deceiving himself who thinks that he can exempt himself from the wages of anguish with which you pay for your pride in being the flower and cream of creation; I understand the enormous truth contained in Goethe's saying: "He who is not prepared for despair is not prepared for life." Courage; you're not the first of those who annihilate themselves, burning in the flame of life as a butterfly burns in the light; you're not the first, you're just one of that rich collection of martyrs who have made of life a beautiful and surprising epic.' "

"Do you know that he explained himself with a certain sort of wisdom?" I said, observing that Paris discoursed on life with a seriousness that, although not free from extravagance, did him, nonetheless, considerable honor.

"That devilish man had begun to philosophize, leaving off his cynical impudence to make reflections in a tone that seemed more mocking to me than his jests of the day before."

"And then what did he do?" I asked, hoping that the ghost would at last take off my friend's dressing gown and slippers, and get dressed and put himself in order.

"You'll see," rejoined the doctor. "I didn't allow anyone to enter that room; but when I wasn't paying attention, a servant came in to announce my father-in-law, Count Torbellino, and he showed no signs of having seen the shadow. The servant apparently thought I was alone. I was going to go out to receive my father-in-law when the latter, who didn't stand on ceremony, came in. I trembled, thinking that he would be able to see Paris; but no. Paris was next to me, and the count didn't see him. In his view, as in the servant's, I was alone in the room. The strangest thing! Several times the ghost passed between him and me, without being seen except by me. Only I heard his footsteps, only I received his glances, indescribably sprightly. But shortly after Count Torbellino had entered, Paris disappeared; I looked to the right and left to see if he was hidden in some corner, but nothing; he had disappeared. I saw only the dressing gown and the slippers, thrown over a chair. My dialogue with my illustrious father-in-law was extremely important, and relating it will be very useful in better understanding this unparalleled story. But first I'm going to give you some background on such a respectable character."

II

"Count Torbellino," continued don Anselmo, "was a tempestuous man, and not because he was irascible, or violent, or given to quarrels, but because his essentially tranquil spirit manifested itself externally in the most resounding and emphatic manner. When he said something stupid, which was fairly often, his voice, naturally harsh, dropped to the lowest pitch of the register; when he wanted to convince someone that he was an important man, engrossed in business matters, his words reached the highest pitch of vain grandiloquence; if he said nothing, his breathing sounded like a far-off storm. Loquacious and pompous, he seemed the symbol of heated discussion, an explosion made man. His listeners were many; guests at his gatherings enjoyed the din of his colossal voice; but when he began to laugh, the crowd of colloquists scattered rapidly, for the good man's laughter dazed and stunned.

"The sonorous box that produced such atrocious noises was proportionate to the sound itself. Corpulent, heavy, cavernous, monumental, the count was an appreciable block who would have done honor to any quarry. Such a mastodon was not lacking in dignity and grace: on the contrary, his rectangular obesity gave him a certain imperial, dictatorial aspect.

"His face was rather more handsome than ugly, laterally decorated with thick salt and pepper sideburns, and the nose had something of the look of a Corinthian volute; the large mouth, with its fleshy, twisted lips, resembled the mouths of those Greek masks that spew forth wreaths and emblems. Two large grimaces held an arrogant hilarity at the corners of this mouth, a hilarity so characteristic of him and so etched in his face, that one might say his smile was a pretense. His glasses were more than that, they were an organ; his forehead, on which some hairs, flattened by his hat and stuck down by sweat, sketched a sort of hieroglyphic inscription, was small, sunken, red; but of an intense and rather transparent red, as though the good man's brains were vermilion or cinnabar. His body was a prodigy of architectural solidity; each extremity, a portent of equilibrium; and his shoulders, his abdomen, and his back, just so many master works of muscular stereometry; his feet, two bricks. In spite of so much solidity, this monolith moved with considerable agility; and when he spoke, his arms waved like two windmill sails, threatening to behead the person who had the misfortune to be listening to him.

44

"As to intelligence, the count was considered ignorant by many and very wise by others; but he was neither the one nor the other. Without being learned, he knew enough to speak about everything, not always talking nonsense. He was, nevertheless, strong in some matters, especially in Politics and Finance. He was very concerned with the rise and fall of public funds, and traded with the credit of the State, taking part with the major capitalists in the riskiest of commercial ventures, which strengthened his knowledge of Finance. His own caused him serious fears, especially in the period of which I'm speaking, and the bad humor caused by his muddled affairs would have turned into hypochondria had not my marriage with his daughter shored up his fortunes.

"He was also distinguished by a notable desire to please people. His kindness, though thundering and explosive, had captured the good will of many. No one had better proof of this kindness than I; I was always the object of his predilection, and I was never more aware of it than on the occasion of which I speak. The count proved to me the great interest he had for me in that dialogue I'm going to relate to you as accurately as my memory permits.

" 'My dear son-in-law,' he said, 'I regret having to speak to you on this head, but it's necessary. Elena can't live this way. Don't be angry: no one knows your good qualities better than I; no one has tried to find excuses for you more than I; but things have reached such a pass...; your temper....!'

" 'I don't understand a word of what you're trying to tell me," I answered him, assuming that something serious was behind those hints.

" 'Everyone in the house says you're crazy,' added the count. 'I am the only one to have argued against this opinion, I, who have known your temperament since before you entered my family. I know that this is not insanity; these fits you've been having are nothing new in you, even if they are being aggravated now by a monomania, by one of those passing states of soul that sometimes put us in such a state that we haven't a shred of sense.'

" 'Well, you'll have to explain all this to me better, if you want me to understand you,' I said, being too confused in my head to grasp all at once the new set of complications my father-in-law was bringing me.

" 'Elena complains, and with reason,' he answered. 'The poor thing has grown so thin these last days that she looks like a corpse. We all try to console her. You really are an odd fish! You torment her in the cruelest manner; you frighten her with your innumerable atrocities. But whom have you ever seen act in such a way? According to what she says, some nights you come into her room like a madman, saying you've heard a man's voice there: at other times, you abuse her, you insult her, swearing you've seen someone jump through the window to the garden. Just when she's most relaxed and calm, you come in furious, shouting and uttering threats and asking where he is; your appearance causes her fear; your words are those of a madman: your manner is overwrought. You shall tell me if there's a woman alive who would have enough strength and spirit to take these things calmly, and consider also if there aren't

45

plenty of reasons in your behavior to draw down upon you not the dislike, but the horror of your wife.'

" 'Yes,' I replied, 'I confess it; but you don't realize that I have my reasons for acting this way.'

" 'Reasons! Don't be stupid. What reasons could you have to act this way? If you had the calm, the philosophy one needs to live in these times in which we find ourselves, this wouldn't happen to you. The problem is that you worry about nothing; you're very punctilious; you take everything to heart, and in sum...you don't know how to live.'

" 'I beg you, my dear father-in-law, to explain that to me, and perhaps it will shed some light on the situation in which I find myself.'

" 'What I mean to say is that you care too much about the opinion of people, something that usually should be despised, especially when, as in the present instance, it's founded on nothing concrete, but on vulgar assumptions, the offspring of great moral decadence.'

" 'But what does public opinion say?' I asked. 'Has someone dared to speak of my house, of my family?...'

" 'I'll tell you what,' he answered emphatically; 'you shouldn't get upset about this, because, aside from the fact that it's unimportant, it's something that's seen all too frequently to cause us any foreboding. There's no need to pay attention to the opinion of those frivolous people who live off gossip and scandal, always spying on a family's most intimate affairs....Don't worry about that. Only with disdain can you answer the vileness of these infamous people who spare nothing, no matter how holy and respectable.'

" 'But what do they say about me?'

" 'Look, we're not going to talk about those things,' he replied, 'I think it's improper even to refer to them. Let's drop the matter, and that's the end of that....Try to be calm.'

" 'No, I want to know, and right now,' I returned agitatedly.

" 'Come now!' exclaimed Count Torbellino, putting on his glasses which had fallen off in the heat of his eloquence. 'You want me to tell you what you know better than I, what has been the cause of all these irrational acts of yours these last days?'

" 'No, I don't know anything. I want to know everything you've suggested to me for my greater confusion.'

" 'Well, it is with indignation that I must tell you, my dear Anselmo, that there have been persons so insolent as to leave open to doubt..., there have been those who have dared to cast aspersions on the virtue of..., of my daughter Elena. I assure you that if I knew who that despicable person was....'

" 'But who, where, what person has said this?' I cried out, terrified upon being faced with the horrible confirmation of what was going on in my head.

46

" 'Who shall know? And the only thing on which they base it is that the young man frequents your house, that young man...the one who's been coming here for some days now..., that Alejandro what's his name.'

" 'I don't know whom you're talking about,' I said, stupefied.

" 'Oh, yes, that man...Why, only yesterday I saw him come in here. I've seen him come in a number of times,' he added, giving me then a description of that infernal being, man, demon, or ghost who had so tormented me under the name of Paris. 'The thing is that as the lad has a reputation for being one of the greatest destroyers of home life ever to have existed, that ever since he's been observed coming in here....'

" 'And who brought this fellow here?'

" 'I don't know. You must know. What's certain is that he visits your house a great deal, and I'm sure Elena treats him as a friend, without suspecting, poor girl, that even though she's innocent, she's bringing about her own dishonor by receiving him. But at the same time, not to receive him would be to justify the treacherous behavior of the gossip mongers, and to some extent to conform to their system. The best thing to do is to scorn all this, my dear Anselmo. You see that I know what the cause of your insanities is, and I can't help but laugh when I consider how you've tormented poor Elena for such a frivolous reason. Be calm, man, be calm, as I've told you before. If just because a couple of despicable characters have talked about you, you go around committing such atrocities, what would you do if you had a real reason?'

"Thus spoke Count Torbellino, and his words, far from shedding some light on the matter, left my head in greater confusion than ever. Before, I had doubted if the figure of Paris was real or merely a figment of my mind, produced by phenomena I didn't understand; this doubt had tormented me greatly. Now, according to the words of my father-in-law, Paris was a real being, known to everyone. Then how had he been seriously wounded by me, recovering afterwards by enchantment without the slightest mark on his body? How did he appear and disappear without my knowing how? This added so greatly to my confusion that when my father-in-law left I sank into involved, labyrinthine cogitation, to see if I could make out a ray of light in all this darkness. My God! It still wasn't enough. To top off my unhappiness, my mother-in-law came in and, using very different arguments from those of her husband, conversed with me for a good space of time.

"My mother-in-law was an old flirt in whom the years had not deadened her desire to please, the foundation stone of her character.

"Having once been extremely beautiful, there was nothing left in her face but pitiful remnants, and only her eyes preserved in their brilliance and expressiveness something of that beauty that had fled, never to return. This disastrous ugliness was offset in part by the complicated painting of her face and by the thousand things she invented to hide the ravages of her person. As to habits, hers were distinguished only by a constant coming and going, which didn't give her a very good reputation, although no one ever said outright that she wasn't honorable. She liked to amuse herself more than most girls who haven't passed twenty; and in this area, the years never made any visible headway against her; for old and all, she never missed a dance, or a comedy, or a stroll, or a gathering, or a ceremony where young, lively people might be found. It seemed as though the years dropped away from her in this pastime, the body renewing itself with the continuous movement.

"This illustrious lady, who held some very strange notions in matters of public opinion, spoke to me in the following manner:

" 'You're a savage, Anselmo, a beast, a tiger. To think that my daughter could live for long in the company of a person like yourself is insanity. If what's happening weren't so bad, it would be absolutely laughable. Really, the frights you give her, showing up in her room like a madman and apparently with your mind deranged because of some wicked idea...! I truly don't know how the poor thing stays alive....She's sick, and I'm afraid her illness may be serious, because frankly, what impressionable, delicate person could long withstand the trials to which you're subjecting her? You absolutely must decide to conduct yourself differently; my daughter can't live this way. Come now, what makes you act the way you do?...I want to know. And when I think that Elena is a model of kindness, of discretion, of prudence! Really, Anselmo, I can see now that there's no greater torture for a young woman than to live with you. No one could find in your company that agreeable confidence that is the foundation of love; you're not kind, far from it; on the contrary, in spite of your good qualities, you make yourself repulsive through your fits of temper, through this misanthropy that consumes you. My daughter will find no tenderness in you, not even those little automatic words of affection which, insignificant in appearance, are extremely important to us, believe me. Besides, it seems you're determined to make her loathe you; you spend your days withdrawn, alone, shut up in this cursed room, where at times they hear you talking as though you were in conversation with the souls of Purgatory.'

" 'They hear me?' I said, listening with terror to that description of my life.

" 'Yes, that's what the servants say,' she went on, laughing, 'they've heard you talking to yourself. Is that what it means to be rational, is that what it means to be a man? Afterwards you come out, and you go shouting off to Elena's room, and she, shaking and scared, watches you search the room as though you were pursuing some shadow. The poor little thing has gotten to the point of being so afraid of you that she trembles just at the sound of your voice. I don't know what's going to come of all this. What a peculiar way you have of treating your wife! You don't keep her company, you don't spoil her, you don't try to amuse her; she's used to being with people, to the pleasures

48

of society..., and to find herself here, alone, closed in...! I'm the only one who cares about her; I've tried to get together a few friends here, to give us a little entertainment, to amuse ourselves a little. But I don't know what it is about this house; it's as gloomy as its owner; everybody flees from it. Lately, almost no one has come, and we would have been very bored if we hadn't been kept company by Alejandro X***.'

" 'Madam, if you please? Who is that gentleman...? I'm quite curious...!' I said animatedly.

" 'For heaven's sake, you've lost your memory as well,' answered my mother-in-law jovially. 'What a state your head is in! So you don't know Alejandro either? He was coming out of here the very moment I was coming in....But he comes here every day....'

" 'Madam, I don't know whom you're talking about.'

" 'But this man is crazy; he no longer knows his best friends; Alejandro X***, who comes to your house so much; the nicest person I've ever had to do with in my life, a friend of yours, as he is of everyone; because that man, I don't know..., he's one of those people who know absolutely everybody.... Of course, he's so nice, so clever, so amusing, discreet, elegant.'

" 'And you say I know him?'

" 'But you're mad! Of course you know him! You've gone out walking a thousand times, you've lunched and dined together, and heaven knows what else...Alejandro, for goodness' sake,' she added, raising her voice as though she were speaking to a deaf man. 'There's no doubt about it, you've lost your mind.'

" 'And you say he keeps you both company?' I asked, at the peak of my stupor.

" 'If it weren't for him, my daughter and I would be very bored. He keeps us company, and he's so nice....He amuses us greatly with his little private stories. Ah! You've no idea how his conversation captivates us, especially Elena, who likes to hear about adventures. That man has travelled à great deal, and even though he's young, he knows the world as though he'd lived centuries.'

" 'And you say I know him?' I asked anxiously.

" 'Heaven help me, what a man! You might as well ask if you know me. You're not well. Anselmo, for heaven's sake, that head of yours....' "

III

"These and other things my mother-in-law and I discussed in that memorable dialogue. She left, for they informed her that Elena had had a fainting fit, and soon afterwards, when I had not yet had time to clear up somewhat the ideas suggested to me by my mother-in-law, a very dear friend of mine entered, who also spoke to me of things I should not pass over in silence, for the sake of a better understanding of this rare occurrence.

" 'I came to inquire about your wife,' he said. 'I've heard that she's ill.'

" 'Yes,' I answered, 'she's not well. She's been sick with something or other for some days now. Who told you?'

" 'I don't remember where I heard it.'

" 'I know they're talking about me,' I pointed out, for I recognized that my friend wanted to tell me something, and that he was hoping that the conversation would come around to it.

" 'They're talking about you? I don't know,' he said, wavering. 'Oh, well, I won't deny it; on the contrary, I'm obligated by our friendship to talk to you about this matter, and the truth is, that's exactly why I've come.'

" 'Go on.'

" 'Of course, there are certain things you should despise; or rather, not despise them altogether; one should take note of them, ponder them, and then decide maturely what one ought to do. This is nothing new. Everyone who occupies a certain position here, like you, is exposed to foolish talk. One must resign oneself, not become furious, because if there's anything that ought to be taken calmly, this is it.'

" 'Calmly!' I replied, losing my own calm completely. 'I am to view my dishonor calmly! I'll seek out the infamous author of this calumny.'

" 'Then you already know about it?'

" 'Yes,' I said; 'I don't know, I've conjectured, I've guessed.'

" 'Well, yes, my friend,' he replied. 'Don't do anything rash. The most solid of reputations is not free from these attacks.'

" 'I swear to you,' I said, 'I'll kill the man who has slandered my house, and whether it be one or many, this vileness will not go unpunished.'

" 'That's bad; it's not done that way. One should deal with Lady Reputation amicably if one doesn't wish to be mistreated by her; one should come to an agreement with the gossips and make certain concessions so they don't malign us completely. To ward off that evil viper, one musn't fight with her; one must flatter her with the sweet sounds of a musical instrument. The venomous crowd is invincible in hand-to-hand combat, and weak when one substitutes astute cunning for a blind defense.'

" 'I can't flatter those scoundrels. My honor is above them.'

" 'That's all very well and good; but one says one thing...well....In these times talk is more to be feared than action. You know how much weight a "they say..." can carry. If you want my advice, go away from here for a while. When you return, it'll all be forgotten. It's the best way you have of freeing yourself from that man, whose continual presence in your house is so harmful to you. That's the best thing; that way it all blows over without a scandal, because scandal, my friend, engraves facts in the public mind, and facts impressed that way are not easily erased.'

" 'But who is this man?' I asked.

" 'Who!' he said in astonishment, amazed that I didn't know him. 'Alejandro X***. I'm sure his visits here have been innocent; but people see him come in, and as he has such a bad reputation....'

" 'Really?' I said, to force him to explain himself more clearly.

" 'Yes,' he replied, 'he's one of those who take pride in their licentious habits. A good figure, graceful, a certain depravity. He has no occupation other than making love, no ambition other than to be the object of the stupid praise of the masses, always delighted at every honor that's lost and every name that's smirched.'

" 'And you say I should leave here?'

" 'Yes: it's urgent. Forget violent measures. Killing, duelling: that all adds to the scandal and the gossip....'

" 'No; I want to kill that man!' I shouted furiously, forgetting for the moment that Paris was immortal.

" 'Kill! Whom? Him? And are you sure that in killing him you'll be punishing a guilty man? You're taking it for granted that there's been a crime, and that's not the issue at hand. It's just a matter of certain rumors which we must suppose to be without any basis whatsoever. Now you tell me if rumors are put down by killing people.'

" 'Well, I can't leave here,' I said, remembering Paris' threat to follow me everywhere; 'he'll come after us.'

" 'How could he go with you?' said my friend. 'And if he does go, it's up to you to keep him from following you for long. Here you can't very easily throw him out of the house without a scandal, but while you're travelling it's more possible to rid yourself of him by any means.'

"We spoke very little more; but what I've related was enough to confuse me more than I already was. The principal theme of my musings was this, which I repeated over and over: 'Then Paris is a real being; the man they call Alejandro is not a shadow, he's not an apparition, he's a man who enters my house and is known to everyone. Alejandro and Paris are two different people; the one I've seen is the representation or imitation of the first.' Tired of that torment, I resolved to go out, to look for the alleviation of this terrible sorrow in the reassurance and advice of people who cared about me. I intended to go to several friends of proven loyalty, and who were moreover very wise in the ways of the world, hoping they could shed some light on this dreadful enigma.

"I went out. According to what I was told later, I wandered along the street with vacant gaze, and unsteady and heavy gait, wearing my hat and clothes in a very odd manner. I made people laugh; and even those who were accustomed to see in me a man not just in the common way stopped as I went past, pointing me out as a curiosity. Although I had determined to consult with certain people, I didn't direct my steps towards any specific place. I went from here to there at random, blindly. Imagine my surprise when, upon crossing some street or other, I stumbled...; I was about to fall, and a hand grasped my arm forcefully. I turned, and it was Paris who was supporting me. I don't know what I felt at that moment. In another state of spirit I would have struck him in the presence of everyone; but that cursed figure now inspired me only with fear: in his presence, my soul took fright, my voice dried up, my forces weakened. From the moment he came to my side, my spirit submitted to the authority of that infernal being, giving in sadly, as though it sensed its inferiority. From that moment, I no longer belonged to myself, I was in his hands, in his power. He took my arm and we walked a long way along the busiest streets without speaking a word. We looked at the people: we met many of my acquaintances along the way, and I noted that as we passed they were whispering, pointing us out. Without knowing how and without my own will having any part in it, that diabolical Paris dragged me towards the Prado, which, as it was one of the loveliest days of autumn, was extremely crowded. The groups drew apart to let us pass, and many of them smiled slyly, observing the two of us. At that instant Paris was visible to all; he was no longer that shadow, perceived only by me, who came out of the canvas of a picture in my room; he was real, and everyone saw him, greeted him, greeted us, watching with malice, though not with surprise, as we walked along together.

"Thus we passed through the Prado; we continued on to Recoletos, without my being able to stop. He dragged me along so, that at times a strange force seemed to be moving my feet. There were more and more people, and the malice was the same on every face I recognized.

"Some people stopped and looked at us for a good while; others seemed to me to be laughing, and all the time we kept walking, walking. I was red with shame; my face burned as though there were live coals on it, and in the bottom of my heart there beat a terrible hatred, a deep sorrow, a dark anguish that could not burst forth, for that demon was pressing it down. Within my chest I felt a sort of hand of fire that squeezed me forcefully, holding in its flaming fist all there was in me of life and feeling....We walked on without resting: huge drops of sweat ran down my forehead, and I felt a great fatigue, although purely mental, for my body was not tired, and I walked along moved by a force within myself I had never had before. We crossed the Castellana, where there were still more people, more acquaintances and more insistence upon staring at us, smiling with a malice that bordered on the insolent. We strolled on, going from one end of the avenue to the other, several times, until dusk was falling, people were leaving, and my soul was covered in mourning; my eyes clouded over, I saw nothing but shadows, and a glacial cold ran through my body. I had to stop: we were at the far end of the avenue; at our backs could be heard the noise of the carriages rumbling off and the footsteps of an occasional straggling promenader. It seems that I then recovered the use of my voice, and I felt a sort of freedom within myself, something like repose, as though the infernal action of that abominable being had ceased to operate on me. I don't know why my gaze was attracted by the extraordinary brilliance of the evening light that, in the West, was dyeing the sky an intense purple.

"I looked at that with a certain pleasure which I had not experienced in a considerable time, and when I turned my eyes to my side, Paris was no longer there, he had dissolved like smoke. Through an easily explained illusion, turning to look to the West, I seemed to see his hated face depicted with flashes of reddish light and violent clouds. I was alone, entirely alone; I had recovered control of myself; but then the mental fatigue I had felt before extended to my body, and I dropped to a bench, lightheaded and exhausted."

IV

"Well, if I'm to speak frankly, my friend don Anselmo," I said, "that adventure, far from becoming clearer as the end approaches, is becoming more complicated and darker. At the beginning, when the figure of Paris appeared to you in your room, the case could be considered a creation of your imagination, a mental aberration. Although rare, there are cases in which a sick imagination produces those phenomena that have no external reality, but exist only within the individual who produces them. The figure that disappeared from the canvas, the voice you thought you heard in Elena's room, the shadow you saw hiding in the well, all that can be explained by an obsession that, though rare, is not impossible. But afterwards it turns out that there is a real being, one Alejandro, a person visible to everyone and who frequents your house; a person exactly like the intrusive shadow and who seems determined to upset marital peace, not by any fantastic means, but by real ones, as can be deduced from your dialogue with your mother-in-law and your friend. What do we agree on? What relationship is there between Paris and Alejandro? By a coincidence I do not think accidental, these are the two names of Helen's ravisher in the heroic fable."

"Now then: you say you didn't know this Alejandro. If you had known him, if before all these apparitions you had been jealous of him, it's understandable that your imagination, overpowered by such an idea, might reach this pathological state that gives rise to such great aberrations. But here the obsession came first, and reality came afterwards to confirm it. Wouldn't it be more logical for reality to come first, and that afterwards, as a result of a real emotional state, these visions that so tormented you should appear?"

"I thought precisely as you say when, having calmed down somewhat, I tried to explain to myself what had happened to me, on the way back to my house. I must tell you that my head had been in a deplorable state since long before all this happened. Besides almost completely losing my memory, there was such an aberration of my senses that I couldn't manage to think straight

53

or to say anything right. I've observed all this afterwards, and I have come to discover, by carefully fathoming the past, something of what existed in my head in that period. After some time had passed, I was able, by dint of remembering, by tying up loose ends, to reconstruct the facts, although not with the clarity they required. Finally, I was able to remember that, in effect, I had known that Alejandro of whom my in-laws, my friend, and all Madrid were talking."

"Well, then, it's all explained," I said. "You worried about that man, you were jealous, you thought about it night and day, and that thought gradually dominated you to the point of occupying your whole spirit: constantly thinking about one idea gave free rein to your fantasy, it weakened your bodily forces with the absolute sway of the spirit, and hence that diseased state that so troubled you. That, although most unusual, happens every day. The mystics who talked of their visions with such faith, believing that they had spoken with Jesus and the Virgin, are proof of that pathological state that gives overwhelming preponderance to imagination above all the other faculties.

"Very well, don Anselmo; think hard and try to remember: before the appearance of Paris, didn't something happen that could be the first, determining cause of that series of phenomena that so agitated you? The truth is that that upset was the result of a previous perturbation. You must say what happened before you saw the painted figure disappear from the canvas."

"Before telling you the end of the adventure," replied don Anselmo, "I'll tell you what I was told by an old friend of my family, an old man whom I had rather forgotten since reaching adulthood. According to him, my father had suffered the same torments, being remarkable among them one in which he was on the verge of losing his life, because the obsessions had deprived him even of the habit of eating and of hunger, sinking him in a deep melancholy. He told me that my father was also pursued by a shadow, although his wasn't a destroyer of marriage, but a fantastic creditor who came to demand enormous sums of money from him, talking to him of a lawsuit that never ended. My father had had an extraordinary horror of legal battles before that: it was his mania, his obsession, his insanity."

"I see it's a family malady," I added. "When one has a natural inclination for a life of fantasy, not to undertake a career as a saint is to miss one's vocation. This unchecked faculty, this rebellious fury that will not submit to the laws of reason, and is not tempered with the influence of good sense, is neither fruitful nor useful for Art. It only serves to produce the raptures and hallucinations of mysticism: it makes of man a being beside himself, who is never within himself, but in another world that he populates as he likes with beings, giving them an incongruous and illogical life, like his own; putting them in action, attributing to them acts as strange, absurd, peculiar as his own."

54

"Well, another friend of mine," continued the doctor, "a worthy scholar I had also known since considerably before all this, told me that this was nothing more than a sickness, and he talked to me of encephalic dislocation, of a certain arrangement of the axes of the little brain cells, polarized by some special means; he also told me that arsenates would work very well on such a pathological state, that the optic nerves had undergone an appreciable change and were producing the images by a process opposite to the normal one, the first sensation starting in the brain and the external impression taking place afterward."

"I don't know anything about medicine," I said, "but there's no doubt that we're dealing here with a disease. I read in the prologue of a book on Neuropathology, which happened to fall into my hands, some very reasonable observations on the effects of fixed ideas on our organism. The author discussed the apprehensions of sick people in a way that I found odd, but not without foundation. He said that if one's attention is constantly fixed on one part of the body, it produces a change in the tissue, and in this way he explained the famous wounds of Saint Francis, which, according to him, were nothing but a lesion produced by the convergence of all the faculties, all the forces of the spirit, toward the point at which they appeared. If fixed ideas produce such tangible effects on animal physiology; if they have sufficient power to change tissue, to alter material, the thing least like it, what might they not do to spiritual life, where all the faculties always work so closely together? I can understand your obsession and your dialogues with that incomprehensible being; I can understand the duel, which was the extreme stage of the hallucination. I understand everything except the lack of real antecedents, of events that would favor this predisposition of yours, setting up the series of psychological phenomena I've mentioned."

"Events, yes; I think there were some," he answered. "The last thing I remember is having heard my wife speak of that young man. I think I saw him too, and spoke to him. But I don't remember anything else. Afterwards, what my mind preserves indelibly is the night when I heard the voice in her room, the disappearance of the figure from the picture, in short, everything I've related to you."

"And you didn't notice if Paris returned to his place?"

"I'll go on. When I returned to my house, I realized, from the moment I entered it, that something was going on. The servants were coming and going in agitation; I heard my mother-in-law's voice, sharp and penetrating, and in the pauses, that of Count Torbellino, hoarse and ringing.

"They informed me immediately that my wife was gravely ill, which was borne out by the presence of two well-known doctors and the consternation of everyone around her. Her illness had become suddenly worse, she had suf-

55

fered a heart attack, and the prognosis, from what the doctors said, was not hopeful. She lay in her bed, suffering rapid changes, now restless and delirious, now exhausted and as though dead. Her mother never stopped talking, lamenting that misfortune in the harshest and shrillest of tones. 'What else can be the cause of this dreadful attack, if not Anselmo's extraordinary behavior? He's driving her into her grave with these incessant humiliations to which he subjects her. It's impossible for a delicate nature to resist that slow torture.' And then she cried with sincere tears, for in spite of being a licentious old coquette, she was not lacking in maternal emotions. Elena became worse and worse. Science was unable to help her, and finally, after watching her suffer horribly for a long period of time, we all realized that she was dying, and that only a miracle could save her."

"And Paris?" I asked, for it seemed strange to me that that devilish seducer should not show up in that final scene, in which he had one of the principal roles.

"Paris? You'll see. That demon was quick to present himself in order to have the final word. The spectacle of Elena's agony so grieved me that I couldn't remain for long in her room. I was unable to look at her without shuddering, feeling a great sorrow together with an intense remorse that my reason could not overcome. When I saw her dying, so beautiful, in the flower of her youth, in the happiest period of her life, I wondered if I, as my mother-in-law said between her sobs, were the only author of this sad end, which she certainly did not deserve. It occurred to me that death is over us all, and chooses us without attending to any arguments we may have to the contrary; but even so, I thought that, had she not been married to me, Elena would not have died so soon. Unable to endure that scene, as I have said, I retired to my room, overwhelmed with grief. There was Paris, sitting down, smoking, tapping his walking stick on the sole of his boot in an absentminded and rather discourteous manner, most incorrect for the present situation of my household. When I came in he turned to me and said:

" 'I'm leaving; you've finally managed it; but at what a price! To be rid of me, you've had to kill her!'

" 'I!' I replied, unable to contain my anger. 'I! You say that I've killed her!'

" 'Yes, you, you've brought her to this pass with your violent actions, your assaults, your sudden raids on her room, with the horror you've inspired in her, with the emotional confusion you've caused her. I've read somewhere, I don't know where, that these shocks, caused by strong impressions and surprise, if frequently repeated so change the body's functions, so unsettle and unbalance it, that at last the normal state is unable to re-establish itself, and death is certain.'

" 'It isn't I, you hateful demon,' I exclaimed. 'It isn't I who have killed her; it's you, you who have brought disorder to this house, who have driven me mad. Your work is to bring mourning and shame; you have dishonored me, you have ruined me, you have wounded me in what I held dearest; you have trodden on my heart, you have jeered at my feelings; you have made hateful to me what I loved most in this world, and of my honor, which was for me of more value than life itself, you have made a joke, an epigram, a bit of gossip in the mouths of the idle and dissolute.'

" 'That is my destiny,' he said, without becoming upset at the insults I hurled at him, and in truth, I was furious and eloquent.

"Without my knowing why, the terror that that demon caused me began to disappear.... Then I said to him:

" 'You are the greatest aberration of society; you're one of those monstrosities that accompany man like a harsh punishment for who knows what crime that we are committing, constantly and without being aware of it.'

" 'Fool!' he exclaimed; 'you called me, you gave me life; I am your handiwork. I will have you remember, although the comparison is an unequal one, the ancient fable of the birth of Minerva. Very well: I emerged from your brain just as that good lady emerged from the brain of Jupiter; I am your idea made man. But don't think because of that that I have no real existence: I walk around, like you, everyone knows me, I'm Mr. so-and-so, just like anyone else. For the public there's an Alejandro, a well-known, renowned man; for you there's this Paris who torments you, this shadow that pursues you, this idea that tortures you. Farewell! I have nothing more to do here; your wife is dying. Adieu!'

"At that moment I heard loud shouts in the interior of the house. Elena had died. Paris disappeared, I felt free, I breathed. I felt as though I hadn't breathed in three days, my chest so enjoyed that restful, healing expansion. At the same time, a deep sorrow filled my soul when I considered the one life less in my house now, when I thought of that spirit that had gone fleeing away from me. At that moment of supreme grief, I seemed to see her pass by like a puff of wind, like a light cloud, but not so wispy or rapid that I couldn't see her features, altered by the mysterious stamp that death puts on even the most beautiful of faces. It passed in front of my eyes, leaving them dazzled for a moment."

"And Alexander?" I asked in the same tone and for the same reason I had asked earlier. "And Paris?"

"That Alexander went to the house the moment he knew of Elena's death, and, from what I heard, the poor man was dismayed and rather tearful. He went to the funeral and to the cemetery, and they told me he even wore mourning for some days."

"That young gentleman," I said, "was the real material expression of that odious Paris who martyred you. He is the real Paris."

"Yes," he assented; "I've seen him often since then, but I've always refused to speak to him. Every time I meet him I shudder. Today he's a licentious old rake, scrofulous and a bit lame. In short: the jealousy that man inspired in me took that form of a vision in my head of which I've told you. It's a strange thing; I was right when I told you that my fantasy was a frantic, savage power, a sickness rather than a faculty."

"The logical order of the story," I said, "is as follows: you knew that that young man was flirting with your wife; you thought about it a great deal, you became absorbed by it, you shut yourself away; the fixed idea gradually took control of you, and finally you went mad, for there's no other way of describing such a horrible delirium."

"Exactly," replied the doctor; "except that I, to give my adventure more truth, I recount it as it happened to me, which is to say, backwards. A complete disorganization took place in my head; and so, when the first of my hallucinations occurred, I didn't remember the background of that painful mental illness."

"And Elena...?" I said, meaning to ask a daring question; but I refrained from fear of wounding the doctor's delicacy.

"I know what you want to ask me," he answered: "you want to know what I think of her conduct, whether or not she was faithful. Over that point I cast a veil; don't make me lift it. I know nothing nor have I tried to find out; I prefer doubt."

After saying this, the doctor fell silent, sinking into his normal reverie. I had nothing more to ask him, and after saying good-night I withdrew, because in spite of the interest he had tried to impart to his narrative, I was so sleepy I could barely keep my eyes open. As I was going downstairs, I remembered that I hadn't asked him something important, something that deserved to be cleared up, that is, if the figure of Paris had shown up again on the canvas, as seemed natural. I thought of going up to have him relieve me of my doubts, satisfying my curiosity; but I hadn't gone two steps when it occurred to me that the case wasn't worth the bother, for it's not very important to me to know it, nor to the reader either.